ROALD DAHL

THE BFG

Illustrated by
Quentin Blake

P9-BUI-966

PUFFIN BOOKS

For Olivia

20 April 1955–17 November 1962

PUFFIN BOOKS
An imprint of Penguin Random House LLC
375 Hudson Street
New York, New York 10014

First published in Great Britain by Jonathan Cape Ltd., 1982
First published in the United States of America by Farrar, Straus, & Giroux, 1982
First published by Puffin Books, 1984
Reprinted by arrangement with Farrar, Straus, & Giroux, LLC
This edition published by Puffin Books, an imprint of Penguin Random House LLC, 2016

Text copyright © 1982 by Roald Dahl
Illustrations copyright © 1982 by Quentin Blake

Penguin supports copyright. Copyright fuels creativity, encourages diverse voices,
promotes free speech, and creates a vibrant culture. Thank you for buying an authorized
edition of this book and for complying with copyright laws by not reproducing, scanning,
or distributing any part of it in any form without permission. You are supporting writers
and allowing Penguin to continue to publish books for every reader.

THE LIBRARY OF CONGRESS HAS CATALOGED THE PREVIOUS PUFFIN BOOKS EDITION
UNDER CATALOG CARD NUMBER: 85-566

This edition ISBN 978-1-101-99769-7

Printed in the United States of America

1 3 5 7 9 10 8 6 4 2

My BFG

When I was a child, every night at bedtime, my father would pace back and forth in the little tiny bedroom I shared with my sister, Ophelia, and tell us wonderful stories of the BFG. We would sit up in bed mesmerized by the tales of our BFG, as we sipped on our witch's potions, which my father always gave us to drink during our "story," as he called it. The witch's potion was a delicious concoction that my father made us every evening at bedtime, a combination of canned peaches or pears, milk, and a few drops of either red, green, or blue food coloring whizzed up in a blender to make a homemade milkshake-type drink. "The witches dropped it off at the doorstep five minutes ago," my father would tell us with convincing authority, the same way he told us about our BFG who lived in a cave under the apple trees of our orchard right next to our house.

Everything was magical, even the witch balls that hung on clear fishing twine at different lengths and heights from our bedroom ceiling. "Witch balls" are beautiful, antique, fragile balls of all different colors. My father told us that they were to keep the bad witches away: *"One look at her reflection in the witch ball and she'll be scared to death and disappear faster than she arrived."* We were safe; we had so many mystical things around us. The Witches (good ones); the BFG; Fantastic Mr. Fox, who lived under the "witch tree," a spectacular beech tree that had grown from three small trees into one massive climbing tree, which stood gracefully halfway up the little country lane where we lived, in a rambling farmhouse called Gipsy House.

The stories were always a surprise—some nights it was the BFG, sometimes it was Fantastic Mr. Fox, sometimes my father told us stories about when he was our age and all the naughty things he and his friends got up to at school, stories he put together later in a book called *Boy*. But what never changed was our evening ritual. After our story (which was never read, always told) was over, my father would take our empty witch's potion glasses, then always ensure that our little window was cracked the tiniest bit. He did this to make sure that later the BFG could get his stick through to blow dreams into our room. Then my father kissed us good night, tucked us in snugly, and turned out our light. Then we waited . . .

The wait was never long. Usually within about five minutes a long bamboo stick slowly poked its way through the middle of our curtains. First the stick would aim at my older sister Ophelia's bed. It stopped steadily for a moment, and then we would hear two terrifically loud blows, rather like the sound a great big whale makes when it blows through its spout. Then, very slowly and carefully, the bamboo stick would turn toward me. The thrill was exhilarating: *what could be my dream tonight?* Two huge blows were exhaled in my direction, and then the long bamboo would slowly retract back through the curtains, and within seconds we went to sleep. We couldn't wait to go to sleep and dream our special dreams that the BFG had made for us that day, from his cave under the apple trees of our orchard.

One evening Ophelia asked my father, "How do we know that you are not making up the BFG?"

"Making him up!" my father said with horror.

"Why can't we go to the window and see him?" I asked.

"Because if you do, he will never come back. He is very shy and does not want anyone to ever see him; his magic might even be stolen by little girls' eyes. The Big Friendly Giant is a magical giant, and magical things are never seen; you just have to believe, and if you don't believe in magic, then you will never find it." We weren't convinced and my father sensed it; yet we believed enough not to go to the window when the bamboo stick came through, just in case.

The very next morning, when we woke up and opened our curtains, all of our doubts were dissolved, as written on our perfectly green lawn were giant brown letters: B.F.G.

We ran downstairs to tell our father, who was extremely annoyed that his prize lawn had been tampered with.

"Now do you believe that the BFG is real?" he asked. "My lawn has been all messed up."

Yes. We believed. And still today, I believe in magic, the BFG, Witches, and Fantastic Foxes; but I also know that late that night, my father had used weed killer to make the giant letters on his precious lawn. The idea of his children believing in magic was far more important than the beautiful grass that he tended with great care.

The day I flew to Vancouver to visit the set of *The BFG*, I can honestly say I felt as though I was Charlie Bucket entering Willy Wonka's chocolate factory. I walked through the large secret doors of the set and suddenly I was in giant land, then Buckingham Palace, then the Queen's bedroom, then the massive dining room at Buckingham Palace. I met Sophie, the Queen, and—the greatest moment of all—I met the BFG. Oh, what a thrill it was—he was kind and beautiful and looked just the way I had always imagined him to look. Even though I am now an adult, I had to fight back tears . . . Tears of pure emotion that everything that I always believed since I was a little girl, but was never allowed to see outside my imagination, was suddenly in front of my very eyes. I could also feel my father walking with me around this enchanting land of giants and dreams. I could hear him telling me, as I walked around in awe, "You see Lukie"—my family nickname—"if you don't believe in magic, you will never find it. You believed and look, you've found it. Isn't it marvelous!"

And yes, marvelous it was. It was probably one of the best days of my entire life. My father was there in spirit; I could feel him, yet I wished more than anything that he could have been there in person with me. He would have been so delighted with absolutely everything, including Melissa Mathison's wonderful script, the fantastic costumes by Joanna Johnston, Rick Carter's production design, Lois Burwell's makeup design, and the hard work of so many other brilliant and creative people who have brought to life, with love and care, our little bedtime story that started out in our tiny bedroom nestled in the English countryside.

I had finally met my BFG. I also met the BFD (Big Friendly Director), Steven Spielberg. I watched in awe as he worked, as he is the only man I have ever met who also believes in magic and giants.

When it was time to say good-bye, I walked through the orphanage dormitory; the little iron beds were all lined up, the room was dark, the beds were perfectly made—with love, with care, and, like everything else I had seen and felt that day, with a little bit of magic.

Lucy Dahl

Contents

The characters in this book are:

HUMANS:

THE QUEEN OF ENGLAND
MARY, the Queen's maid
MR TIBBS, the Palace butler
THE HEAD OF THE ARMY
THE HEAD OF THE AIR FORCE
And, of course, SOPHIE, *an orphan*

GIANTS:

THE FLESHLUMPEATER
THE BONECRUNCHER
THE MANHUGGER
THE CHILDCHEWER
THE MEATDRIPPER
THE GIZZARDGULPER
THE MAIDMASHER
THE BLOODBOTTLER
THE BUTCHER BOY
And, of course, THE BFG

The Witching Hour

Sophie couldn't sleep.

A brilliant moonbeam was slanting through a gap in the curtains. It was shining right on to her pillow.

The other children in the dormitory had been asleep for hours.

Sophie closed her eyes and lay quite still. She tried very hard to doze off.

It was no good. The moonbeam was like a silver blade slicing through the room on to her face.

The house was absolutely silent. No voices came up from downstairs. There were no footsteps on the floor above either.

The window behind the curtain was wide open, but nobody was walking on the pavement outside. No cars went by on the street. Not the tiniest sound could be heard anywhere. Sophie had never known such a silence.

Perhaps, she told herself, this was what they called the witching hour.

The witching hour, somebody had once whispered to her, was a special moment in the middle of the night when every child and every grown-up was in a deep deep sleep, and all the dark things came out from hiding and had the world to themselves.

The moonbeam was brighter than ever on Sophie's pillow. She decided to get out of bed and close the gap in the curtains.

You got punished if you were caught out of bed after lights-out. Even if you said you had to go to the lavatory, that was not accepted as an excuse and they punished you just the same. But there was no one about now, Sophie was sure of that.

She reached out for her glasses that lay on the chair beside her bed. They had steel rims and very thick lenses, and she could hardly see a thing without them. She put them on, then she slipped out of bed and tip-toed over to the window.

When she reached the curtains, Sophie hesitated. She longed to duck underneath them and lean out of the window to see what the world looked like now that the witching hour was at hand.

She listened again. Everywhere it was deathly still.

The longing to look out became so strong she couldn't resist it. Quickly, she ducked under the curtains and leaned out of the window.

In the silvery moonlight, the village street she knew so well seemed completely different. The houses looked bent and crooked, like houses in a fairy tale. Everything was pale and ghostly and milky-white.

Across the road, she could see Mrs Rance's shop, where you bought buttons and wool and bits of elastic. It didn't look real. There was something dim and misty about that too.

Sophie allowed her eye to travel further and further down the street.

Suddenly she froze. *There was something coming up the street on the opposite side.*

It was something black ...

Something tall and black ...

Something very tall and very black and very thin.

Who?

It wasn't a human. It couldn't be. It was four times as tall as the tallest human. It was so tall its head was higher than the upstairs windows of the houses. Sophie opened her mouth to scream, but no sound came out. Her throat, like her whole body, was frozen with fright.

This was the witching hour all right.

The tall black figure was coming her way. It was keeping very close to the houses across the street, hiding in the shadowy places where there was no moonlight.

On and on it came, nearer and nearer. But it was moving in spurts. It would stop, then it would move on, then it would stop again.

But what on earth was it doing?

Ah-ha! Sophie could see now what it was up to. It was stopping in front of each house. It would stop and peer into the upstairs window of each house in the street. It actually had to bend down to peer into the upstairs windows. That's how tall it was.

It would stop and peer in. Then it would slide on to the next house and stop again, and peer in, and so on all along the street.

It was much closer now and Sophie could see it more clearly.

Looking at it carefully, she decided it *had* to be some

kind of PERSON. Obviously it was not a human. But it was definitely a PERSON.

A GIANT PERSON, perhaps.

Sophie stared hard across the misty moonlit street. The Giant (if that was what he was) was wearing a long BLACK CLOAK.

In one hand he was holding what looked like a VERY LONG, THIN TRUMPET.

In the other hand, he held a LARGE SUITCASE.

The Giant had stopped now right in front of Mr and Mrs Goochey's house. The Goocheys had a greengrocer's shop in the middle of the High Street, and the family lived above the shop. The two Goochey children slept in the upstairs front room, Sophie knew that.

The Giant was peering through the window into the room where Michael and Jane Goochey were sleeping. From across the street, Sophie watched and held her breath.

She saw the Giant step back a pace and put the suitcase down on the pavement. He bent over and opened the suitcase. He took something out of it. It looked like a glass jar, one of those square ones with a screw top. He unscrewed the top of the jar and poured what was in it into the end of the long trumpet thing.

Sophie watched, trembling.

She saw the Giant straighten up again and she saw him poke the trumpet in through the open upstairs window of the room where the Goochey children were sleeping. She saw the Giant take a deep breath and *whoof*, he blew through the trumpet.

No noise came out, but it was obvious to Sophie that whatever had been in the jar had now been blown through the trumpet into the Goochey children's bedroom.

What could it be?

As the Giant withdrew the trumpet from the window and bent down to pick up the suitcase he happened to turn his head and glance across the street.

In the moonlight, Sophie caught a glimpse of an enormous long pale wrinkly face with the most enormous ears. The nose was as sharp as a knife, and above the nose there were two bright flashing eyes, and the eyes were staring straight at Sophie. There was a fierce and devilish look about them.

Sophie gave a yelp and pulled back from the window. She flew across the dormitory and jumped into her bed and hid under the blanket.

And there she crouched, still as a mouse, and tingling all over.

The Snatch

Under the blanket, Sophie waited.

After a minute or so, she lifted a corner of the blanket and peeped out.

For the second time that night her blood froze to ice and she wanted to scream, but no sound came out. There at the window, with the curtains pushed aside, was the enormous long pale wrinkly face of the Giant Person, staring in. The flashing black eyes were fixed on Sophie's bed.

The next moment, a huge hand with pale fingers came snaking in through the window. This was followed by an arm, an arm as thick as a tree-trunk, and the arm, the hand, the fingers were reaching out across the room towards Sophie's bed.

This time Sophie really did scream, but only for a second because very quickly the huge hand clamped down over her blanket and the scream was smothered by the bedclothes.

Sophie, crouching underneath the blanket, felt strong fingers grasping hold of her, and then she was lifted up from her bed, blanket and all, and whisked out of the window.

If you can think of anything more terrifying than that happening to you in the middle of the night, then let's hear about it.

The awful thing was that Sophie knew exactly what was going on although she couldn't see it happening. She knew that a Monster (or Giant) with an enormous long pale wrinkly face and dangerous eyes had plucked her from her bed in the middle of the witching hour and was now carrying her out through the window smothered in a blanket.

What actually happened next was this. When the Giant had got Sophie outside, he arranged the blanket so that he could grasp all the four corners of it at once in one of his huge hands, with Sophie imprisoned inside. In the other hand he seized the suitcase and the long trumpet thing and off he ran.

Sophie, by squirming around inside the blanket, managed to push the top of her head out through a little gap just below the Giant's hand. She stared around her.

She saw the village houses rushing by on both sides. The Giant was sprinting down the High Street. He was running so fast his black cloak was streaming out behind

him like the wings of a bird. Each stride he took was as long as a tennis court. Out of the village he ran, and soon they were racing across the moonlit fields. The hedges dividing the fields were no problem to the Giant. He simply strode over them. A wide river appeared in his path. He crossed it in one flying stride.

Sophie crouched in the blanket, peering out. She was being bumped against the Giant's leg like a sack of potatoes. Over the fields and hedges and rivers they went, and after a while a frightening thought came into Sophie's head. *The Giant is running fast*, she told herself, *because he is hungry and he wants to get home as quickly as possible, and then he'll have me for breakfast.*

The Cave

The Giant ran on and on. But now a curious change took place in his way of running. He seemed suddenly to go into a higher gear. Faster and faster he went and soon he was travelling at such a speed that the landscape became blurred. The wind stung Sophie's cheeks. It made her eyes water. It whipped her head back and whistled in her ears. She could no longer feel the Giant's feet touching the ground. She had a weird sensation they were flying. It was impossible to tell whether they were over land or sea. This Giant had some sort of magic in his legs. The wind rushing against Sophie's face became so strong that she had to duck down again into the blanket to prevent her head from being blown away.

Was it really possible that they were crossing oceans? It certainly felt that way to Sophie. She crouched in the blanket and listened to the howling of the wind. It went on for what seemed like hours.

Then all at once the wind stopped its howling. The pace began to slow down. Sophie could feel the Giant's feet pounding once again over the earth. She poked her head up out of the blanket to have a look. They were in a country of thick forests and rushing rivers. The Giant had definitely slowed down and was now running more normally, although normal was a silly word to use to describe a galloping giant. He leaped over a dozen rivers. He went rattling through a great forest, then down into a valley and up over a range of hills as bare as concrete, and soon he was galloping over a desolate wasteland that was not quite of this earth. The ground was flat and pale yellow. Great lumps of blue rock were scattered around,

and dead trees stood everywhere like skeletons. The moon had long since disappeared and now the dawn was breaking.

Sophie, still peering out from the blanket, saw suddenly ahead of her a great craggy mountain. The mountain was dark blue and all around it the sky was gushing and glistening with light. Bits of pale gold were flying among delicate frosty-white flakes of cloud, and over to one side the rim of the morning sun was coming up red as blood.

Right beneath the mountain, the Giant stopped. He was puffing mightily. His great chest was heaving in and out. He paused to catch his breath.

Directly in front of them, lying against the side of the mountain, Sophie could see a massive round stone. It was as big as a house. The Giant reached out and rolled the stone to one side as easily as if it had been a football, and now, where the stone had been, there appeared a vast black hole. The hole was so large the Giant didn't even have to duck his head as he went in. He strode into the black hole still carrying Sophie in one hand, the trumpet and the suitcase in the other.

As soon as he was inside, he stopped and turned and rolled the great stone back into place so that the entrance to his secret cave was completely hidden from outside.

Now that the entrance had been sealed up, there was not a glint of light inside the cave. All was black.

Sophie felt herself being lowered to the ground. Then the Giant let go of the blanket completely. His footsteps moved away. Sophie sat there in the dark, shivering with fear.

He is getting ready to eat me, she told herself. He will probably eat me raw, just as I am.

Or perhaps he will boil me first.

Or he will have me fried. He will drop me like a rasher of bacon into some gigantic frying-pan sizzling with fat.

A blaze of light suddenly lit up the whole place. Sophie blinked and stared.

She saw an enormous cavern with a high rocky roof.

The walls on either side were lined with shelves, and on the shelves there stood row upon row of glass jars. There were jars everywhere. They were piled up in the corners. They filled every nook and cranny of the cave.

In the middle of the floor there was a table twelve feet high and a chair to match.

The Giant took off his black cloak and hung it against the wall. Sophie saw that under the cloak he was wearing a sort of collarless shirt and a dirty old leather waistcoat that didn't seem to have any buttons. His trousers were faded green and were far too short in the legs. On his bare feet he was wearing a pair of ridiculous sandals that for some reason had holes cut along each side, with a large hole at the end where his toes stuck out. Sophie, crouching on the floor of the cave in her nightie, gazed back at him through thick steel-rimmed glasses. She was trembling like a leaf in the wind, and a finger of ice was running up and down the length of her spine.

'Ha!' shouted the Giant, walking forward and rubbing his hands together. 'What has us got here?' His booming voice rolled around the walls of the cave like a burst of thunder.

The BFG

The Giant picked up the trembling Sophie with one hand and carried her across the cave and put her on the table.

Now he really is going to eat me, Sophie thought.

The Giant sat down and stared hard at Sophie. He had truly enormous ears. Each one was as big as the wheel of a truck and he seemed to be able to move them inwards and outwards from his head as he wished.

'I is hungry!' the Giant boomed. He grinned, showing massive square teeth. The teeth were very white and very square and they sat in his mouth like huge slices of white bread.

'P . . . please don't eat me,' Sophie stammered.

The Giant let out a bellow of laughter. 'Just because I is a giant, you think I is a man-gobbling cannybull!' he shouted. 'You is about right! Giants is all cannybully and murderful! And they *does* gobble up human beans! We is in Giant Country now! Giants is everywhere around! Out there us has the famous Bonecrunching Giant! Bonecrunching Giant crunches up two whoppsy-whiffling human beans for supper every night! Noise is earbursting! Noise of crunching bones goes crackety-crack for miles around!'

'Owch!' Sophie said.

'Bonecrunching Giant only gobbles human beans from

Turkey,' the Giant said. 'Every night Bonecruncher is galloping off to Turkey to gobble Turks.'

Sophie's sense of patriotism was suddenly so bruised by this remark that she became quite angry. 'Why Turks?' she blurted out. 'What's wrong with the English?'

'Bonecrunching Giant says Turks is tasting oh ever so much juicier and more scrumdiddlyumptious! Bonecruncher says Turkish human beans has a glamourly flavour. He says Turks from Turkey is tasting of turkey.'

'I suppose they would,' Sophie said.

'Of course they would!' the Giant shouted. 'Every human bean is diddly and different. Some is scrumdiddlyumptious and some is uckyslush. Greeks is all full of uckyslush. No giant is eating Greeks, ever.'

'Why not?' Sophie asked.

'Greeks from Greece is all tasting greasy,' the Giant said.

'I imagine that's possible too,' Sophie said. She was wondering with a bit of a tremble what all this talking about eating people was leading up to. Whatever happened, she simply *must* play along with this peculiar giant and smile at his jokes.

But were they jokes? Perhaps the great brute was just working up an appetite by talking about food.

'As I am saying,' the Giant went on, 'all human beans is having different flavours. Human beans from Panama is tasting very strong of hats.'

'Why hats?' Sophie said.

'You is not very clever,' the Giant said, moving his great ears in and out. 'I thought all human beans is full of brains, but your head is emptier than a bundongle.'

'Do you like vegetables?' Sophie asked, hoping to steer

the conversation towards a slightly less dangerous kind of food.

'You is trying to change the subject,' the Giant said sternly. 'We is having an interesting babblement about the taste of the human bean. The human bean is not a vegetable.'

'Oh, but the bean *is* a vegetable,' Sophie said.

'Not the *human* bean,' the Giant said. 'The human bean has two legs and a vegetable has no legs at all.'

Sophie didn't argue any more. The last thing she wanted to do was to make the Giant cross.

'The human bean,' the Giant went on, 'is coming in dillions of different flavours. For instance, human beans from Wales is tasting very whooshey of fish. There is something very fishy about Wales.'

'You mean *whales*,' Sophie said. 'Wales is something quite different.'

'Wales is whales,' the Giant said. 'Don't gobblefunk around with words. I will now give you another example. Human beans from Jersey has a most disgustable woolly tickle on the tongue,' the Giant said. 'Human beans from Jersey is tasting of cardigans.'

'You mean jerseys,' Sophie said.

'You are once again gobblefunking!' the Giant shouted. 'Don't do it! This is a serious and snitching subject. May I continue?'

'Please do,' Sophie said.

'Danes from Denmark is tasting ever so much of dogs,' the Giant went on.

'Of course,' Sophie said. 'They taste of great danes.'

'Wrong!' cried the Giant, slapping his thigh. 'Danes

from Denmark is tasting doggy because they is tasting of
labradors!'

'Then what do the people of Labrador taste of?'
Sophie asked.

'Danes,' the Giant cried, triumphantly. 'Great danes!'

'Aren't you getting a bit mixed up?' Sophie said.

'I is a very mixed up Giant,' the Giant said. 'But I does
do my best. And I is not nearly as mixed up as the other
giants. I know one who gallops all the way to Wellington
for his supper.'

'Wellington?' Sophie said. 'Where is Wellington?'

'Your head is full of squashed flies,' the Giant said. 'Wellington is in New Zealand. The human beans in Wellington has an especially scrumdiddlyumptious taste, so says the Welly-eating Giant.'

'What do the people of Wellington taste of?' Sophie asked.

'Boots,' the Giant said.

'Of course,' Sophie said. 'I should have known.'

Sophie decided that this conversation had now gone on long enough. If she was going to be eaten, she'd rather get it over and done with right away than be kept hanging around any more. 'What sort of human beings do *you* eat?' she asked, trembling.

'*Me!*' shouted the Giant, his mighty voice making the glass jars rattle on their shelves. 'Me gobbling up human beans! This I never! The others, yes! All the others is gobbling them up every night, but not me! I is a freaky Giant! I is a nice and jumbly Giant! I is the only nice and jumbly Giant in Giant Country! I is THE BIG FRIENDLY GIANT! I is the BFG. What is *your* name?'

'My name is Sophie,' Sophie said, hardly daring to believe the good news she had just heard.

The Giants

'But if you are so nice and friendly,' Sophie said, 'then why did you snatch me from my bed and run away with me?'

'Because you SAW me,' the Big Friendly Giant answered. 'If anyone is ever SEEING a giant, he or she must be taken away hipswitch.'

'Why?' asked Sophie.

'Well, first of all,' said the BFG, 'human beans is not really *believing* in giants, is they? Human beans is not *thinking* we exist.'

'I do,' Sophie said.

'Ah, but that is only because you has SEEN me!' cried the BFG. 'I cannot possibly allow *anyone*, even little girls, to be SEEING me and staying at home. The first thing you would be doing, you would be scuddling around yodelling the news that you were actually SEEING a giant, and then a great giant-hunt, a mighty giant look-see, would be starting up all over the world, with the human beans all rummaging for the great giant you saw and getting wildly excited. People would be coming rushing and bushing after me with goodness knows what and they would be catching me and locking me into a cage to be stared at. They would be putting me into the zoo or the bunkumhouse with all those squiggling hippodumplings and crocadowndillies.'

Sophie knew that what the Giant said was true. If any person reported actually having seen a giant haunting the streets of a town at night, there would most certainly be a terrific hullabaloo across the world.

'I will bet you,' the BFG went on, 'that *you* would have been splashing the news all over the wonky world, wouldn't you, if I hadn't wiggled you away?'

'I suppose I would,' Sophie said.

'And that would never do,' said the BFG.

'So what will happen to me now?' Sophie asked.

'If you do go back, you will be telling the world,' said the BFG, 'most likely on the telly-telly bunkum box and the radio squeaker. So you will just have to be staying here with me for the rest of your life.'

'Oh no!' cried Sophie.

'Oh yes!' said the BFG. 'But I am warning you not

ever to go whiffling about out of this cave without I is
with you or you will be coming to an ucky-mucky end! I
is showing you now who is going to eat you up if they is
ever catching even one tiny little glimp of you.'

The Big Friendly Giant picked Sophie off the table and
carried her to the cave entrance. He rolled the huge stone
to one side and said, 'Peep out over there, little girl, and
tell me what you is seeing.'

Sophie, sitting on the BFG's hand, peeped out of the
cave.

The sun was up now and shining fiery-hot over the
great yellow wasteland with its blue rocks and dead trees.

'Is you seeing them?' the BFG asked.

Sophie, squinting through the glare of the sun, saw
several tremendous tall figures moving among the rocks

about five hundred yards away. Three or four others were sitting quite motionless on the rocks themselves.

'This is Giant Country,' the BFG said. 'Those is all giants, every one.'

It was a brain-boggling sight. The giants were all naked except for a sort of short skirt around their waists, and their skins were burnt by the sun. But it was the sheer size of each one of them that boggled Sophie's brain most of all. They were simply colossal, far taller and wider than the Big Friendly Giant upon whose hand she was now sitting. And oh how ugly they were! Many of them had large bellies. All of them had long arms and big feet. They were too far away for their faces to be seen clearly, and perhaps that was a good thing.

'What on earth are they doing?' Sophie asked.

'Nothing,' said the BFG. 'They is just moocheling and footcheling around and waiting for the night to come. Then they will all be galloping off to places where *people* is living to find their suppers.'

'You mean to Turkey,' Sophie said.

'Bonecrunching Giant will be galloping to Turkey, of course,' said the BFG. 'But the others will be whiffling off to all sorts of flungaway places like Wellington for the booty flavour and Panama for the hatty taste. Every giant is having his own favourite hunting ground.'

'Do they ever go to England?' Sophie asked.

'Often,' said the BFG. 'They say the English is tasting ever so wonderfully of crodscollop.'

'I'm not sure I quite know what that means,' Sophie said.

'Meanings is not important,' said the BFG. 'I cannot be right all the time. Quite often I is left instead of right.'

34

'And are all those beastly giants over there really going off again tonight to eat people?' Sophie asked.

'All of them is guzzling human beans every night,' the BFG answered. 'All of them excepting me. That is why you will be coming to an ucky-mucky end if any of them should ever be getting his gogglers upon you. You would be swalloped up like a piece of frumpkin pie, all in one dollop!'

'But eating people is horrible!' Sophie cried. 'It's frightful! Why doesn't someone stop them?'

'And who please is going to be stopping them?' asked the BFG.

'Couldn't you?' said Sophie.

'Never in a pig's whistle!' cried the BFG. 'All of those

35

man-eating giants is enormous and very fierce! They is all at least two times my wideness and double my royal highness!'

'Twice as high as you!' cried Sophie.

'Easily that,' said the BFG. 'You is seeing them in the distance but just wait till you get them close up. Those giants is all at least fifty feet tall with huge muscles and cockles alive alive-o. I is the titchy one. I is the runt. Twenty-four feet is puddlenuts in Giant Country.'

'You mustn't feel bad about it,' Sophie said. 'I think you are just great. Why even your toes must be as big as sausages.'

'Bigger,' said the BFG, looking pleased. 'They is as big as bumplehammers.'

'How many giants are there out there?' Sophie asked.

'Nine altogether,' answered the BFG.

'That means,' said Sophie, 'that somewhere in the world, every single night, nine wretched people get carried away and eaten alive.'

'More,' said the BFG. 'It is all depending, you see, on how big the human beans is. Japanese beans is very small, so a giant will need to gobble up about six Japanese before he is feeling full up. Others like the Norway people and the Yankee-Doodles is ever so much bigger and usually two or three of those makes a good tuck-in.'

'But do these disgusting giants go to every single country in the world?' Sophie asked.

'All countries excepting Greece is getting visited some time or another,' the BFG answered. 'The country which a giant visits is depending on how he is feeling. If it is very warm weather and a giant is feeling as hot as a sizzlepan, he will probably go galloping far up to the frisby north to get himself an Esquimo or two to cool him down. A nice fat Esquimo to a giant is like a lovely ice-cream lolly to you.'

'I'll take your word for it,' Sophie said.

'And then again, if it is a frotsy night and the giant is fridging with cold, he will probably point his nose towards the swultering hotlands to guzzle a few Hotten-tots to warm him up.'

'How perfectly horrible,' Sophie said.

'Nothing hots a cold giant up like a hot Hottentot,' the BFG said.

'And if you were to put me down on the ground and I was to walk out among them now,' Sophie said, 'would they really eat me up?'

'Like a whiffswiddle!' cried the BFG. 'And what is more, you is so small they wouldn't even have to chew you. The first one to be seeing you would pick you up in his fingers and down you'd go like a drop of drain-water!'

'Let's go back inside,' Sophie said. 'I hate even watching them.'

The Marvellous Ears

Back in the cave, the Big Friendly Giant sat Sophie down once again on the enormous table. 'Is you quite snuggly there in your nightie?' he asked. 'You isn't fridgy cold?'

'I'm fine,' Sophie said.

'I cannot help thinking,' said the BFG, 'about your poor mother and father. By now they must be jipping and skumping all over the house shouting "Hello hello where is Sophie gone?"'

'I don't have a mother and father,' Sophie said. 'They both died when I was a baby.'

'Oh, you poor little scrumplet!' cried the BFG. 'Is you not missing them very badly?'

'Not really,' Sophie said, 'because I never knew them.'

'You is making me sad,' the BFG said, rubbing his eyes.

'Don't be sad,' Sophie said. 'No one is going to be worrying too much about me. That place you took me from was the village orphanage. We are all orphans in there.'

'You is a norphan?'

'Yes.'

'How many is there in there?'

'Ten of us,' Sophie said. 'All little girls.'

'Was you happy there?' the BFG asked.

'I hated it,' Sophie said. 'The woman who ran it was

called Mrs Clonkers and if she caught you breaking any of the rules, like getting out of bed at night or not folding up your clothes, you got punished.'

'How is you getting punished?'

'She locked us in the dark cellar for a day and a night without anything to eat or drink.'

'The rotten old rotrasper!' cried the BFG.

'It was horrid,' Sophie said. 'We used to dread it. There were rats down there. We could hear them creeping about.'

'The filthy old fizzwiggler!' shouted the BFG. 'That is the horridest thing I is hearing for years! You is making me sadder than ever!' All at once, a huge tear that would have filled a bucket rolled down one of the BFG's cheeks and fell with a splash on the floor. It made quite a puddle.

Sophie watched with astonishment. What a strange and moody creature this is, she thought. One moment he is telling me my head is full of squashed flies and the next moment his heart is melting for me because Mrs Clonkers locks us in the cellar.

'The thing that worries *me*,' Sophie said, 'is having to stay in this dreadful place for the rest of my life. The orphanage was pretty awful, but I wouldn't have been there for ever, would I?'

'All is my fault,' the BFG said. 'I is the one who kidsnatched you.' Yet another enormous tear welled from his eye and splashed on to the floor.

'Now I come to think of it, I won't actually be here all that long,' Sophie said.

'I is afraid you will,' the BFG said.

'No, I won't,' Sophie said. 'Those brutes out there are bound to catch me sooner or later and have me for tea.'

'I is *never* letting that happen,' the BFG said.

For a few moments the cave was silent. Then Sophie said, 'May I ask you a question?'

The BFG wiped the tears from his eyes with the back of his hand and gave Sophie a long thoughtful stare. 'Shoot away,' he said.

'Would you please tell me what you were doing in our village last night? Why were you poking that long trumpet thing into the Goochey children's bedroom and then blowing through it?'

'Ah-ha!' cried the BFG, sitting up suddenly in his chair. 'Now we is getting nosier than a parker!'

'And the suitcase you were carrying,' Sophie said. 'What on earth was *that* all about?'

The BFG stared suspiciously at the small girl sitting cross-legged on the table.

'You is asking me to tell you whoppsy big secrets,' he said. 'Secrets that nobody is ever hearing before.'

'I won't tell a soul,' Sophie said. 'I swear it. How could I anyway? I am stuck here for the rest of my life.'

'You could be telling the other giants.'

'No, I couldn't,' Sophie said. 'You told me they would eat me up the moment they saw me.'

'And so they would,' said the BFG. 'You is a human bean and human beans is like strawbunkles and cream to those giants.'

'If they are going to eat me the moment they see me, then I wouldn't have time to tell them anything, would I?' Sophie said.

'You wouldn't,' said the BFG.

'Then why did you say I might?'

'Because I is brimful of buzzburgers,' the BFG said.

'If you listen to everything I am saying you will be getting earache.'

'Please tell me what you were doing in our village,' Sophie said. 'I promise you can trust me.'

'Would you teach me how to make an elefunt?' the BFG asked.

'What *do* you mean?' Sophie said.

'I would dearly love to have an elefunt to ride on,' the BFG said dreamily. 'I would so much love to have a jumbly big elefunt and go riding through green forests picking peachy fruits off the trees all day long. This is a sizzling-hot muckfrumping country we is living in. Nothing grows in it except snozzcumbers. I would love to go somewhere else and pick peachy fruits in the early morning from the back of an elefunt.'

Sophie was quite moved by this curious statement.

'Perhaps one day we will get you an elephant,' she said. 'And peachy fruits as well. Now tell me what you were doing in our village.'

'If you is really wanting to know what I am doing in your village,' the BFG said, 'I is blowing a dream into the bedroom of those children.'

'*Blowing a dream?*' Sophie said. 'What *do* you mean?'

'I is a dream-blowing giant,' the BFG said. 'When all the other giants is galloping off every what way and which to swollop human beans, I is scuddling away to other places to blow dreams into the bedrooms of sleeping children. Nice dreams. Lovely golden dreams. Dreams that is giving the dreamers a happy time.'

'Now hang on a minute,' Sophie said. 'Where do you get these dreams?'

'I collect them,' the BFG said, waving an arm towards

41

all the rows and rows of bottles on the shelves. 'I has billions of them.'

'You can't *collect* a dream,' Sophie said. 'A dream isn't something you can catch hold of.'

'You is never going to understand about it,' the BFG said. 'That is why I is not wishing to tell you.'

'Oh, please tell me!' Sophie said. 'I *will* understand! Go on! Tell me how you collect dreams! Tell me everything!'

The BFG settled himself comfortably in his chair and crossed his legs. 'Dreams,' he said, 'is very mysterious things. They is floating around in the air like little wispy-misty bubbles. And all the time they is searching for sleeping people.'

'Can you see them?' Sophie asked.

'Never at first.'

'Then how do you catch them if you can't see them?' Sophie asked.

'Ah-ha,' said the BFG. 'Now we is getting on to the dark and dusky secrets.'

'I won't tell a soul.'

'I is trusting you,' the BFG said. He closed his eyes and sat quite still for a moment, while Sophie waited.

'A dream,' he said, 'as it goes whiffling through the night air, is making a tiny little buzzing-humming noise. But this little buzzy-hum is so silvery soft, it is impossible for a human bean to be hearing it.'

'Can *you* hear it?' Sophie asked.

The BFG pointed up at his enormous truck-wheel ears which he now began to move in and out. He performed this exercise proudly, with a little proud smile on his face. 'Is you seeing these?' he asked.

'How could I miss them?' Sophie said.

'They maybe is looking a bit propsposterous to you,'
the BFG said, 'but you must believe me when I say they
is very extra-usual ears indeed. They is not to be coughed
at.'

'I'm quite sure they're not,' Sophie said.

'They is allowing me to hear absolutely every single
twiddly little thing.'

'You mean you can hear things I can't hear?' Sophie
said.

'You is *deaf as a dumpling* compared with me!' cried the
BFG. 'You is hearing only thumping loud noises with
those little earwigs of yours. But I am hearing *all the secret
whisperings of the world!*'

'Such as what?' Sophie asked.

43

'In your country,' he said, 'I is hearing the footsteps of a ladybird as she goes walking across a leaf.'

'*Honestly?*' Sophie said, beginning to be impressed.

'What's more, I is hearing those footsteps *very loud*,' the BFG said. 'When a ladybird is walking across a leaf, I is hearing her feet going *clumpety-clumpety-clump* like giants' footsteps.'

'Good gracious me!' Sophie said. 'What else can you hear?'

'I is hearing the little ants chittering to each other as they scuddle around in the soil.'

'You mean you can hear ants talking?'

'Every single word,' the BFG said. 'Although I is not exactly understanding their langwitch.'

'Go on,' Sophie said.

'Sometimes, on a very clear night,' the BFG said, 'and if I is swiggling my ears in the right direction,' – and here he swivelled his great ears upwards so they were facing the ceiling – 'if I is swiggling them like this and the night is very clear, I is sometimes hearing faraway music coming from the stars in the sky.'

A queer little shiver passed through Sophie's body. She sat very quiet, waiting for more.

'My ears is what told me you was watching me out of your window last night,' the BFG said.

'But I didn't make a sound,' Sophie said.

'I was hearing your heart beating across the road,' the BFG said. 'Loud as a drum.'

'Go on,' Sophie said. 'Please.'

'I can hear plants and trees.'

'Do *they* talk?' Sophie asked.

'They is not exactly talking,' the BFG said. 'But they

44

is making noises. For instance, if I come along and I is picking a lovely flower, if I is twisting the stem of the flower till it breaks, then the plant is screaming. I can hear it screaming and screaming very clear.'

'You don't mean it!' Sophie cried. 'How awful!'

'It is screaming just like you would be screaming if someone was twisting *your* arm right off.'

'Is that really true?' Sophie asked.

'You think I is swizzfiggling you?'

'It *is* rather hard to believe.'

'Then I is stopping right here,' said the BFG sharply. 'I is not wishing to be called a fibster.'

'Oh no! I'm not calling you anything!' Sophie cried. 'I believe you! I do really! Please go on!'

The BFG gave her a long hard stare. Sophie looked right back at him, her face open to his. 'I believe you,' she said softly.

She had offended him, she could see that.

'I wouldn't ever be fibbling to you,' he said.

'I know you wouldn't,' Sophie said. 'But you must understand that it isn't easy to believe such amazing things straightaway.'

'I understand that,' the BFG said.

'So do please forgive me and go on,' she said.

He waited a while longer, and then he said, 'It is the same with trees as it is with flowers. If I is chopping an axe into the trunk of a big tree, I is hearing a terrible sound coming from inside the heart of the tree.'

'What sort of sound?' Sophie asked.

'A soft moaning sound,' the BFG said. 'It is like the sound an old man is making when he is dying slowly.'

He paused. The cave was very silent.

45

'Trees is living and growing just like you and me,' he said. 'They is alive. So is plants.'

He was sitting very straight in his chair now, his hands clasped tightly together in front of him. His face was bright, his eyes round and bright as two stars.

'Such wonderful and terrible sounds I is hearing!' he said. 'Some of them you would never wish to be hearing yourself! But some is like glorious music!'

He seemed almost to be transfigured by the excitement of his thoughts. His face was beautiful in its blaze of emotions.

'Tell me some more about them,' Sophie said quietly.

'You just ought to be hearing the little micies talking!' he said. 'Little micies is always talking to each other and I is hearing them as loud as my own voice.'

'What do they say?' Sophie asked.

'Only the micies know that,' he said. 'Spiders is also talking a great deal. You might not be thinking it but spiders is the most tremendous natterboxes. And when they is spinning their webs, they is singing all the time. They is singing sweeter than a nightingull.'

'Who else do you hear?' Sophie asked.

'One of the biggest chatbags is the cattlepiddlers,' the BFG said.

'What do they say?'

'They is argying all the time about who is going to be the prettiest butteryfly. That is all they is ever talking about.'

'Is there a dream floating around in here now?' Sophie asked.

The BFG moved his great ears this way and that, listening intently. He shook his head. 'There is no dream

46

in here,' he said, 'except in the bottles. I has a special place to go for catching dreams. They is not often coming to Giant Country.'

'How do you catch them?'

'The same way you is catching butteryflies,' the BFG answered. 'With a net.' He stood up and crossed over to a corner of the cave where a pole was leaning against the wall. The pole was about thirty feet long and there was a net on the end of it. 'Here is the dream-catcher,' he said, grasping the pole in one hand. 'Every morning I is going out and snitching new dreams to put in my bottles.'

Suddenly, he seemed to lose interest in the conversation. 'I is getting hungry,' he said. 'It is time for eats.'

Snozzcumbers

'But if you don't eat people like all the others,' Sophie said, 'then what *do* you live on?'

'That is a squelching tricky problem around here,' the BFG answered. 'In this sloshflunking Giant Country, happy eats like pineapples and pigwinkles is simply not growing. Nothing is growing except for one extremely icky-poo vegetable. It is called the snozzcumber.'

'The snozzcumber!' cried Sophie. 'There's no such thing.'

The BFG looked at Sophie and smiled, showing about twenty of his square white teeth. 'Yesterday,' he said, 'we was not believing in giants, was we? Today we is not believing in snozzcumbers. Just because we happen not to have actually *seen* something with our own two little winkles, we think it is not existing. What about for instance the great squizzly scotch-hopper?'

'I beg your pardon?' Sophie said.

'And the humplecrimp?'

'What's that?' Sophie said.

'And the wraprascal?'

'The what?' Sophie said.

'And the crumpscoddle?'

'Are they animals?' Sophie asked.

'They is *common* animals,' said the BFG contemptuously. 'I is not a very know-all giant myself, but it seems to me that you is an absolutely know-nothing human bean. Your brain is full of rotten-wool.'

'You mean cotton-wool,' Sophie said.

'What I mean and what I say is two different things,' the BFG announced rather grandly. 'I will now show you a snozzcumber.'

The BFG flung open a massive cupboard and took out the weirdest-looking thing Sophie had ever seen. It was about half as long again as an ordinary man but was much thicker. It was as thick around its girth as a perambulator. It was black with white stripes along its length. And it was covered all over with coarse knobbles.

'Here is the repulsant snozzcumber!' cried the BFG, waving it about. 'I squoggle it! I mispise it! I dispunge it! But because I is refusing to gobble up human beans like the other giants, I must spend my life guzzling up icky-poo snozzcumbers instead. If I don't, I will be nothing but skin and groans.'

'You mean skin and *bones*,' Sophie said.

'I *know* it is bones,' the BFG said. 'But please understand that I cannot be helping it if I sometimes is saying things a little squiggly. I is trying my very best all the time.' The Big Friendly Giant looked suddenly so forlorn that Sophie got quite upset.

'I'm sorry,' she said. 'I didn't mean to be rude.'

'There never was any schools to teach me talking in Giant Country,' the BFG said sadly.

'But couldn't your mother have taught you?' Sophie asked.

'My *mother!*' cried the BFG. 'Giants don't have mothers! Surely you is knowing *that*.'

'I did *not* know that,' Sophie said.

'Whoever heard of a *woman* giant!' shouted the BFG, waving the snozzcumber around his head like a lasso. 'There never was a woman giant! And there never will be one. Giants is always men!'

Sophie felt herself getting a little muddled. 'In that case,' she said, 'how were you born?'

'Giants isn't born,' the BFG answered. 'Giants *appears* and that's all there is to it. They simply *appears*, the same way as the sun and the stars.'

'And when did you appear?' Sophie asked.

'Now how on earth could I be knowing a thing like that?' said the BFG. 'It was so long ago I couldn't count.'

'You mean you don't even know how *old* you are?'

'No giant is knowing that,' the BFG said. 'All I is knowing about myself is that I is very old, very very old and crumply. Perhaps as old as the earth.'

'What happens when a giant dies?' Sophie asked.

'Giants is never dying,' the BFG answered. 'Sometimes and quite suddenly, a giant is disappearing and nobody is ever knowing where he goes to. But mostly us giants is simply going on and on like whiffsy time-twiddlers.'

The BFG was still holding the awesome snozzcumber in his right hand, and now he put one end into his mouth and bit off a huge hunk of it. He started crunching it up and the noise he made was like the crunching of lumps of ice.

'It's filthing!' he spluttered, speaking with his mouth full and spraying large pieces of snozzcumber like bullets in Sophie's direction. Sophie hopped around on the table-top, ducking out of the way.

'It's disgusterous!' the BFG gurgled. 'It's sickable! It's rotsome! It's maggotwise! Try it yourself, this foulsome snozzcumber!'

'No, thank you,' Sophie said, backing away.

'It's all you're going to be guzzling around here from now on so you might as well get used to it,' said the BFG. 'Go on, you snipsy little winkle, have a go!'

Sophie took a small nibble. 'Uggggggggh!' she spluttered. 'Oh no! Oh gosh! Oh help!' She spat it out quickly. 'It tastes of frogskins!' she gasped. 'And rotten fish!'

'Worse than that!' cried the BFG, roaring with laughter. 'To me it is tasting of clockcoaches and slime-wanglers!'

51

'Do we really have to eat it?' Sophie said.

'You do unless you is wanting to become so thin you will be disappearing into a thick ear.'

'Into *thin air*,' Sophie said. 'A thick ear is something quite different.'

Once again that sad winsome look came into the

BFG's eyes. 'Words,' he said, 'is oh such a twitch-tickling problem to me all my life. So you must simply try to be patient and stop squibbling. As I am telling you before, I know exactly what words I am wanting to say, but somehow or other they is always getting squiff-squiddled around.'

'That happens to everyone,' Sophie said.

'Not like it happens to me,' the BFG said. 'I is speaking the most terrible wigglish.'

'I think you speak beautifully,' Sophie said.

'You do?' cried the BFG, suddenly brightening. 'You really do?'

'Simply beautifully,' Sophie repeated.

'Well, that is the nicest present anybody is ever giving me in my whole life!' cried the BFG. 'Are you sure you is not twiddling my leg?'

'Of course not,' Sophie said. 'I just love the way you talk.'

'How wondercrump!' cried the BFG, still beaming. 'How whoopsey-splunkers! How absolutely squiffling! I is all of a stutter.'

'Listen,' Sophie said. 'We don't *have* to eat snozzcumbers. In the fields around our village there are all sorts of lovely vegetables like cauliflowers and carrots. Why don't you get some of those next time you go visiting?'

The BFG raised his great head proudly in the air. 'I is a very honourable giant,' he said. 'I would rather be chewing up rotsome snozzcumbers than snitching things from other people.'

'You stole *me*,' Sophie said.

'I did not steal you very much,' said the BFG, smiling gently. 'After all, you is only a tiny little girl.'

The Bloodbottler

Suddenly, a tremendous thumping noise came from outside the cave entrance and a voice like thunder shouted, 'Runt! Is you there, Runt? I is hearing you jabbeling! Who is you jabbeling to, Runt?'

'Look out!' cried the BFG. 'It's the Bloodbottler!' But before he had finished speaking, the stone was rolled aside and a fifty-foot giant, more than twice as tall and wide as the BFG, came striding into the cave. He was naked except for a dirty little piece of cloth around his bottom.

Sophie was on the table-top. The enormous partly eaten snozzcumber was lying near her. She ducked behind it.

The creature came clumping into the cave and stood towering over the BFG. 'Who was you jabbeling to in here just now?' he boomed.

'I is jabbeling to myself,' the BFG answered.

'Pilfflefizz!' shouted the Bloodbottler. 'Bugswallop!' he boomed. 'You is talking to a human bean, that's what I is thinking!'

'No no!' cried the BFG.

'Yus yus!' boomed the Bloodbottler. 'I is guessing you has snitched away a human bean and brought it back to your bunghole as a pet! So now I is winkling it out and guzzling it as extra snacks before my supper!'

The poor BFG was very nervous. 'There's n-no one in here,' he stammered. 'W-why don't you l-leave me alone?'

The Bloodbottler pointed a finger as large as a tree-trunk at the BFG. 'Runty little scumscrewer!' he shouted. 'Piffling little swishfiggler! Squimpy little bottle-wart! Prunty little pogswizzler! I is now going to search the primroses!' He grabbed the BFG by the arm. 'And you is going to help me do it. Us together is going to winkle out this tasteful little human bean!' he shouted.

The BFG had intended to whisk Sophie off the table as soon as he got the chance and hide her behind his back, but now there was no hope of doing this. Sophie peered around the chewed-off end of the enormous snozz-cumber, watching the two giants as they moved away down the cave. The Bloodbottler was a gruesome sight. His skin was reddish-pink. There was black hair sprout-ing on his chest and arms and on his stomach. The hair on his head was long and dark and tangled. His foul face was round and squashy-looking. The eyes were tiny black holes. The nose was small. But the mouth was huge. It spread right across the face almost ear to ear, and it had lips that were like two gigantic purple frankfurters lying one on top of the other. Craggy yellow teeth stuck out between the two purple frankfurter lips, and rivers of spit ran down over the chin.

It was not in the least difficult to believe that this ghastly brute ate men, women and children every night.

The Bloodbottler, still holding the BFG by the arm, was examining the rows and rows of bottles. 'You and your pibbling bottles!' he shouted. 'What is you putting in them?'

'Nothing that would interest you,' the BFG answered.

'You is only interested in guzzling human beans.'

'And you is dotty as a dogswoggler!' cried the Blood-bottler.

Soon the Bloodbottler would be coming back, Sophie told herself, and he was bound to search the table-top. But she couldn't possibly jump off the table. It was twelve feet high. She'd break a leg. The snozzcumber, although it was as thick as a perambulator, was not going to hide her if the Bloodbottler picked it up. She examined the chewed-off end. It had large seeds in the middle, each one as big as a melon. They were embedded in soft slimy stuff. Taking care to stay out of sight, Sophie reached forward and scooped away half a dozen of these seeds. This left a hole in the middle of the snozzcumber large enough for her to crouch in so long as she rolled herself up into a ball. She crawled into it. It was a wet and slimy hiding-place, but what did that matter if it was going to save her from being eaten.

The Bloodbottler and the BFG were coming back towards the table now. The BFG was nearly fainting with fear. Any moment, he was telling himself, Sophie would be discovered and eaten.

Suddenly, the Bloodbottler grabbed the half-eaten snozzcumber. The BFG stared at the bare table. Sophie, where is you? he thought desperately. You cannot possibly be jumpelling off that high table, so where is you hiding, Sophie?

'So this is the filthing rotsome glubbage you is eating!' boomed the Bloodbottler, holding up the partly eaten snozzcumber. 'You must be cockles to be guzzling such rubbsquash!'

For a moment, the Bloodbottler seemed to have forgotten about his search for Sophie. The BFG decided to lead him further off the track. 'That is the scrumdiddlyumptious snozzcumber,' he said. 'I is guzzling it gleefully every night and day. Is you never trying a snozzcumber, Bloodbottler?'

'Human beans is juicier,' the Bloodbottler said.

'You is talking rommytot,' the BFG said, growing braver by the second. He was thinking that if only he could get the Bloodbottler to take one bite of the repulsive vegetable, the sheer foulness of its flavour would send him bellowing out of the cave. 'I is happy to let you sample it,' the BFG went on. 'But please, when you see how truly glumptious it is, do not be guzzling the whole thing. Leave me a little snitchet for my supper.'

The Bloodbottler stared suspiciously with small piggy eyes at the snozzcumber.

Sophie, crouching inside the chewed-off end, began to tremble all over.

'You is not switchfiddling me, is you?' said the Bloodbottler.

'Never!' cried the BFG passionately. 'Take a bite and I am positive you will be shouting out oh how scrumdiddlyumptious this wonderveg is!'

The BFG could see the greedy Bloodbottler's mouth beginning to water more than ever at the prospect of extra food. 'Vegitibbles is very good for you,' he went on. 'It is not healthsome always to be eating meaty things.'

'Just this once,' the Bloodbottler said, 'I is going to taste these rotsome eats of yours. But I is warning you that if it is filthsome, I is smashing it over your sludgy little head!'

He picked up the snozzcumber.

59

He began raising it on its long journey to his mouth, some fifty feet up in the air.

Sophie wanted to scream *Don't!* But that would have been an even more certain death. Crouching among the slimy seeds, she felt herself being lifted up and up and up.

Suddenly, there was a *crunch* as the Bloodbottler bit a huge hunk off the end. Sophie saw his yellow teeth clamping together, a few inches from her head. Then there was utter darkness. She was in his mouth. She caught a whiff of his evil-smelling breath. It stank of bad meat. She waited for the teeth to go *crunch* once more. She prayed that she would be killed quickly.

'*Eeeeeowtch!*' roared the Bloodbottler. 'Ughbwelch! Ieeeech!' And then he spat.

All of the great lumps of snozzcumber that were in his mouth, as well as Sophie herself, went shooting out across the cave.

If Sophie had struck the stony wall of the cave, she would most certainly have been killed. Instead, she hit the soft folds of the BFG's black cloak hanging against the wall. She dropped to the ground, half-stunned. She crawled under the hem of the cloak and there she crouched.

'You little swinebuggler!' roared the Bloodbottler. 'You little pigswiller!' He rushed at the BFG and smashed what was left of the snozzcumber over his head. Fragments of the filthy vegetable splashed all over the cave.

'You is not loving it?' the BFG asked innocently, rubbing his head.

'Loving it!' yelled the Bloodbottler. 'That is the most disgusterous taste that is ever touching my teeth! You

must be buggles to be swalloping slutch like that! Every night you could be galloping off happy as a hamburger and gobbling juicy human beans!'

'Eating human beans is wrong and evil,' the BFG said.

'It is guzzly and glumptious!' shouted the Blood-bottler. 'And tonight I is galloping off to Chile to swobble a few human Chile beans. Is you wishing to know why I is choosing Chile?'

'I is not wishing to know anything,' the BFG said, very dignified.

'I is choosing Chile,' the Bloodbottler said, 'because I is fed up with the taste of Esquimos. It is important I has plenty of cold eats in this scuddling hot weather, and the next coldest thing to an Esquimo is a Chile bean. Human beans from Chile is very chilly.'

'Horrible,' the BFG said. 'You ought to be ashamed.'

'Other giants is all saying they is wanting to gallop off to England tonight to guzzle school-chiddlers,' the

Bloodbottler said. 'I is very fond indeed of English school-chiddlers. They has a nice inky-booky flavour. Perhaps I will change my mind and go to England with them.'

'You is disgusting,' the BFG said.

'And you is an insult to the giant peoples!' shouted the Bloodbottler. 'You is not fit to be a giant! You is a squinky little squiddler! You is a pibbling little pitsqueak! You is a . . . cream puffnut!'

With that, the horrible Bloodbottling Giant strode out of the cave. The BFG ran to the cave entrance and quickly rolled the stone back into place.

'Sophie,' he whispered. 'Sophie, where is you, Sophie?'

Sophie emerged from under the hem of the black cloak. 'I'm here,' she said.

The BFG picked her up and held her tenderly in the palm of his hand. 'Oh, I is so happy to be finding you all in one lump!' he said.

'I was in his mouth,' Sophie said.

'You was *what!*' cried the BFG.

Sophie told him what had happened.

'And there I was telling him to eat the filthsome snozz-cumber and you was all the time inside it!' the BFG cried.

'Not much fun,' Sophie said.

'Just look at you, you poor little chiddler!' cried the BFG. 'You is all covered in snozzcumber and giant spit.' He set about cleaning her up as best he could. 'I is hating those other giants more than ever now,' he said. 'You know what I should like?'

'What?' Sophie said.

'I should like to find a way of disappearing them, every single one.'

'I'd be glad to help you,' Sophie said. 'Let me see if I can't think up a way of doing it.'

Frobscottle and Whizzpoppers

By now Sophie was beginning to feel not only extremely hungry, but very thirsty as well. Had she been at home she would have finished her breakfast long ago.

'Are you sure there's nothing else to eat around here except those disgusting smelly snozzcumbers?' she asked.

'Not even a fizzwinkel,' answered the Big Friendly Giant.

'In that case, may I please have a little water?' she said.

'Water?' said the BFG, frowning mightily. 'What is water?'

'We drink it,' Sophie said. 'What do you drink?'

'Frobscottle,' announced the BFG. 'All giants is drinking frobscottle.'

'Is it as nasty as your snozzcumbers?' Sophie asked.

'Nasty!' cried the BFG. 'Never is it nasty! Frobscottle is sweet and jumbly!' He got up from his chair and went to a second huge cupboard. He opened it and took out a glass bottle that must have been six feet tall. The liquid inside it was pale green, and the bottle was half full.

'Here is frobscottle!' he cried, holding the bottle up proud and high, as though it contained some rare wine. 'Delumptious fizzy frobscottle!' he shouted. He gave it a shake and the green stuff began to fizz like mad.

'But look! It's fizzing the *wrong way!*' Sophie cried. And indeed it was. The bubbles, instead of travelling upwards

and bursting on the surface, were shooting downwards and bursting at the bottom. A pale green frothy fizz was forming at the bottom of the bottle.

'What on earth is you meaning *the wrong way?*' asked the BFG.

'In our fizzy drinks,' Sophie said, 'the bubbles always go up and burst at the top.'

'*Upwards* is the *wrong way!*' cried the BFG. 'You mustn't ever be having the bubbles going upwards! That the most flushbunking rubbish I ever is hearing!'

'Why do you say that?' Sophie asked.

'You is asking me *why?*' cried the BFG, waving the enormous bottle around as though he were conducting an orchestra. 'You is actually meaning to tell me you cannot see *why* it is a scrotty mistake to have the bubbles flying up instead of down?'

'You said it was flushbunking. Now you say it's scrotty. Which is it?' Sophie asked politely.

'Both!' cried the BFG. 'It is a flushbunking *and* a scrotty mistake to let the bubbles go upwards! If you can't see why, you must be as quacky as a duckhound! By ringo, your head must be so full of frogsquinkers and buzzwangles, I is frittered if I know how you can think at all!'

'Why shouldn't the bubbles go upward?' Sophie asked.

'I will explain,' said the BFG. 'But tell me first what name is you calling *your* frobscottle by?'

'One is Coke,' Sophie said. 'Another is Pepsi. There are lots of them.'

'And the bubbles is *all* going up?'

'They all go up,' Sophie said.

'Catasterous!' cried the BFG. 'Upgoing bubbles is a catasterous disastrophe!'

'Will you *please* tell me why?' Sophie said.

'If you will listen carefully I will try to explain,' said the BFG. 'But your brain is so full of bugwhiffles, I doubt you will ever understand.'

'I'll do my best,' Sophie said patiently.

'Very well, then. When you is drinking this cokey drink of yours,' said the BFG, 'it is going straight down into your tummy. Is that right? Or is it left?'

'It's right,' Sophie said.

'And the *bubbles* is going also into your tummy. Right or left?'

'Right again,' Sophie said.

'And the bubbles is fizzing upwards?'

'Of course,' Sophie said.

'Which means,' said the BFG, 'that they will all come swishwiffling up your throat and out of your mouth and make a foulsome belchy burp!'

66

'That is often true,' Sophie said. 'But what's wrong with a little burp now and again? It's sort of fun.'

'Burping is filthsome,' the BFG said. 'Us giants is never doing it.'

'But with *your* drink,' Sophie said, 'what was it you called it?'

'Frobscottle,' said the BFG.

'With frobscottle,' Sophie said, 'the bubbles in your tummy will be going *downwards* and that could have a far nastier result.'

'Why nasty?' asked the BFG, frowning.

'Because,' Sophie said, blushing a little, 'if they go down instead of up, they'll be coming out somewhere else with an even louder and ruder noise.'

'A whizzpopper!' cried the BFG, beaming at her. 'Us giants is making whizzpoppers all the time! Whizzpopping is a sign of happiness. It is music in our ears! You surely is not telling me that a little whizzpopping is forbidden among human beans?'

'It is considered extremely rude,' Sophie said.

'But you is whizzpopping, is you not, now and again?' asked the BFG.

'Everyone is whizzpopping, if that's what you call it,' Sophie said. 'Kings and Queens are whizzpopping. Presidents are whizzpopping. Glamorous film stars are whizzpopping. Little babies are whizzpopping. But where I come from, it is not polite to talk about it.'

'Redunculous!' said the BFG. 'If everyone is making whizzpoppers, then why not talk about it? We is now having a swiggle of this delicious frobscottle and you will see the happy result.' The BFG shook the bottle vigorously. The pale green stuff fizzed and bubbled. He

67

removed the cork and took a tremendous gurgling swig.

'It's glummy!' he cried. 'I love it!'

For a few moments, the Big Friendly Giant stood quite still, and a look of absolute ecstasy began to spread over his long wrinkly face. Then suddenly the heavens opened and he let fly with a series of the loudest and rudest noises Sophie had ever heard in her life. They reverberated around the walls of the cave like thunder and the glass jars rattled on their shelves. But most astonishing of all, the force of the explosions actually lifted the enormous giant clear off his feet, like a rocket.

'*Whoopee!*' he cried, when he came down to earth again. 'Now *that* is whizzpopping for you!'

Sophie burst out laughing. She couldn't help it.

'Have some yourself!' cried the BFG, tipping the neck of the enormous bottle towards her.

'Don't you have a cup?' Sophie said.

'No cups. Only bottle.'

Sophie opened her mouth, and very gently the BFG tipped the bottle forward and poured some of the fabulous frobscottle down her throat.

And oh gosh, how delicious it was! It was sweet and refreshing. It tasted of vanilla and cream, with just the faintest trace of raspberries on the edge of the flavour. And the bubbles were wonderful. Sophie could actually feel them bouncing and bursting all around her tummy. It was an amazing sensation. It felt as though hundreds of tiny people were dancing a jig inside her and tickling her with their toes. It was lovely.

'It's lovely!' she cried.

'Just wait,' said the BFG, flapping his ears.

Sophie could feel the bubbles travelling lower and

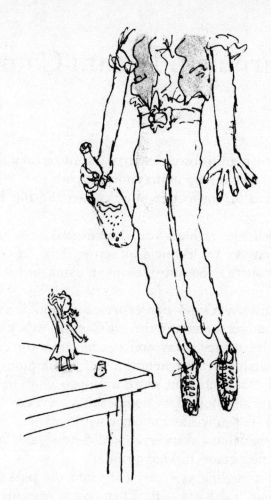

lower down her tummy, and then suddenly, inevitably ... the explosion came. The trumpets sounded and she too made the walls of the cavern ring with the sound of music and thunder.

'Bravo!' shouted the BFG, waving the bottle. 'You is very good for a beginner! Let's have some more!'

Journey to Dream Country

After the mad frobscottle party was over, Sophie settled herself again on top of the enormous table.

'You is feeling better now?' asked the Big Friendly Giant.

'Much better, thank you,' Sophie said.

'Whenever I is feeling a bit scrotty,' the BFG said, 'a few gollops of frobscottle is always making me hopscotchy again.'

'I must say it's quite an experience,' Sophie said.

'It's a razztwizzler,' the BFG said. 'It's gloriumptious.' He turned away and strode across the cave and picked up his dream-catching net. 'I is galloping off now,' he said, 'to catch some more whoppsy-whiffling dreams for my collection. I is doing this every day without missing. Is you wishing to come with me?'

'Not me, thank you very much!' Sophie said. 'Not with those other giants lurking outside!'

'I is snuggling you very cosy into the pocket of my waistcoat,' the BFG said. 'Then no one is seeing you.'

Before Sophie could protest, he had picked her up off the table and popped her into the waistcoat pocket. There was plenty of room in there. 'Is you wishing for a little hole to peep out from?' he asked her.

'There's one here already,' she said. She had found a small hole in the pocket, and when she put one eye close to it, she could see out very well indeed. She watched the BFG as he bent down and filled his suitcase with empty glass jars. He closed the lid, picked up the suitcase in one hand, took the pole with the net on the end in the other hand, and marched towards the entrance of the cave.

As soon as he was outside, the BFG set off across the great hot yellow wasteland where the blue rocks lay and the dead trees stood and where all the other giants were skulking about.

Sophie, squatting low on her heels in the pocket of the leather waistcoat, had one eye glued to the little hole. She saw the group of enormous giants about three hundred yards ahead.

'Hold your breaths!' the BFG whispered down to her. 'Cross your figglers! Here we go! We is going right past all these other giants! Is you seeing that whopping great one, the one nearest to us?'

'I see him,' Sophie whispered back, quivering.

'That is the horriblest of them all. And the biggest of them all. He is called the Fleshlumpeating Giant.'

'I don't want to hear about him,' Sophie said.

'He is fifty-four feet high,' the BFG said softly as he jogged along. 'And he is swolloping human beans like they is sugar-lumps, two or three at a time.'

'You're making me nervous,' Sophie said.

'I is nervous myself,' the BFG whispered. 'I always gets as jumpsy as a joghopper when the Fleshlumpeating Giant is around.'

'Keep away from him,' Sophie pleaded.

'Not possible,' the BFG answered. 'He is galloping easily two times as quicksy as me.'

'Shall we turn back?' Sophie said.

71

'Turning back is worse,' the BFG said. 'If they is seeing me running away, they is all giving chase and throwing rocks.'

'They would never *eat* you though would they?' Sophie asked.

'Giants is never guzzling other giants,' the BFG said. 'They is fighting and squarreling a lot with each other, but never guzzling. Human beans is more tasty to them.'

The giants had already spotted the BFG and all heads were turned, watching him as he jogged forward. He was aiming to pass well to the right of the group.

Through her little peep-hole, Sophie saw the Fleshlumpeating Giant moving over to intercept them. He didn't hurry. He just loped over casually to a point where the BFG would have to pass. The others loped after him. Sophie counted nine of them altogether and she recognized the Bloodbottler in the middle of them. They were bored. They had nothing to do until nightfall. There was an air of menace about them as they loped slowly across the plain with long lolloping strides, heading for the BFG.

'Here comes the runty one!' boomed the Fleshlumpeater. 'Ho-ho there, runty one! Where is you splatchwinkling away to in such a hefty hurry?' He shot out an enormous arm and grabbed the BFG by the hair. The BFG didn't struggle. He simply stopped and stood quite still and said, 'Be so kind as to be letting go of my hair, Fleshlumpeater.'

The Fleshlumpeater released him and stepped back a pace. The other giants stood around, waiting for the fun to start.

'Now then, you little grobsquiffler!' boomed the Fleshlumpeater. 'We is all of us wanting to know where you is galloping off to every day in the daytime. Nobody ought to be galloping off to anywhere until it is getting dark. The human beans could easily be spotting you and starting a giant hunt and we is not wanting that to happen, is we not?'

'We is not!' shouted the other giants. 'Go back to your cave, runty one!'

'I is not galloping to any human bean country,' the BFG said. 'I is going to other places.'

'I is thinking,' said the Fleshlumpeater, 'that you is catching human beans and keeping them as pets!'

'Right you is!' cried the Bloodbottler. 'Just now I is hearing him chittering away to one of them in his cave!'

'You is welcome to go and search my cave from frack to bunt,' the BFG answered. 'You can go looking into every crook and nanny. There is no human beans or stringy beans or runner beans or jelly beans or any other beans in there.'

Sophie crouched still as a mouse inside the BFG's pocket. She hardly dared breathe. She was terrified she might sneeze. The slightest sound or movement would give her away. Through the tiny peep-hole she watched the giants clustering around the poor BFG. How revolting they were! All of them had piggy little eyes and enormous mouths. When the Fleshlumpeater was speaking, she got a glimpse of his tongue. It was jet black, like a slab of black steak. Every one of them was more than twice as tall as the BFG.

Suddenly, the Fleshlumpeater shot out two enormous

73

hands and grabbled the BFG around the waist. He tossed him high in the air and shouted, 'Catch him, Manhugger!'

The Manhugger caught him. The other giants spread out quickly in a large circle, each giant about twenty yards from his neighbour, preparing for the game they were going to play. Now the Manhugger threw the BFG high and far, shouting 'Catch him, Bonecruncher!'

The Bonecruncher ran forward and caught the tumbling BFG and immediately swung him up again. 'Catch him, Childchewer!' he shouted.

And so it went on. The giants were playing ball with the BFG, vying with each other to see who could throw him the highest. Sophie dug her nails into the sides of the pocket, trying to prevent herself from tumbling out when she was upside down. She felt as though she were in a barrel going over the Niagara Falls. And all the time there was the fearful danger that one of the giants would fail to catch the BFG and he would go crashing to the ground.

'Catch him, Meatdripper!' . . .

'Catch him, Gizzardgulper!' . . .

'Catch him, Maidmasher!' ...
'Catch him, Bloodbottler!' ...
'Catch him! ... Catch him! ... Catch him! ...'
In the end, they got bored with this game. They
dumped the poor BFG on the ground. He was dazed and
shattered. They gave him a few kicks and shouted, 'Run,
you little runt! Let us be seeing how fast you is galloping!'
The BFG ran. What else could he do? The giants picked
up rocks and hurled them after him. He managed to
dodge them. 'Ruddy little runt!' they shouted. 'Troggy
little twit! Shrivelly little shrimp! Mucky little midget!

Squaggy little squib! Grobby little grub!'

At last the BFG got clear of them all and in another couple of minutes the pack of giants was out of sight over the horizon. Sophie popped her head up from the pocket. 'I didn't like that,' she said.

'Phew!' said the BFG. 'Phew and far between! They was in a nasty crotching mood today, was they not! I is sorry you was having such a whirlgig time.'

'No worse than you,' Sophie said. 'Would they ever *really* hurt you?'

'I isn't ever trusting them,' the BFG said.

'How do they actually catch the humans they eat?' Sophie asked.

'They is usually just sticking an arm in through the bedroom window and snitching them from their beds,' the BFG said.

'Like you did to me.'

'Ah, but I isn't eating you,' the BFG said.

'How else do they catch them?' Sophie asked.

'Sometimes,' the BFG said, 'they is swimmeling in from the sea like fishies with only their heads showing above the water, and then out comes a big hairy hand and grabbles someone off the beach.'

'Children as well?'

'Often chiddlers,' the BFG said. 'Little chiddlers who is building sandcastles on the beach. That is who the swimmeling ones are after. Little chiddlers is not so tough to eat as old grandmamma, so says the Childchewing Giant.'

As they talked, the BFG was galloping fast over the land. Sophie was standing right up in his waistcoat pocket now and holding on to the edge with both hands.

Her head and shoulders were in the open and the wind was blowing in her hair.

'How else do they catch people?' she asked.

'All of them is having their own special ways of catching the human bean,' the BFG said. 'The Meatdripping Giant is preferring to pretend he is a big tree growing in the park. He is standing in the park in the dusky evening and he is holding great big branches over his head, and there he is waiting until some happy families is coming to have a picnic under the spreading tree. The Meatdripping giant is watching them as they lay out their little picnic. But in the end it is the Meatdripper who is having the picnic.'

'It's too awful!' Sophie cried.

'The Gizzardgulping Giant is a city lover,' the BFG went on. 'The Gizzardgulper is lying high up between the roofs of houses in the big cities. He is lying there snuggy as a sniggler and watching the human beans walking on the street below, and when he sees one that looks like it has a whoppsy-good flavour, he grabs it. He is simply reaching down and snitching it off the street like a monkey taking a nut. He says it is nice to be able to pick and choose what you is having for your supper. He says it is like choosing from a menu.'

'Don't people *see* him doing it?' Sophie asked.

'Never is they seeing him. Do not forget it is dusky-dark at this time. Also, the Gizzardgulper has a very fast arm. His arm is going up and down quicker than squinkers.'

'But if all these people are disappearing every night, surely there's some sort of an outcry?' Sophie said.

'The world is a whopping big place,' the BFG said. 'It has a hundred different countries. The giants is clever.

They is careful not to be skididdling off to the same country too often. They is always switchfiddling around.'

'Even so . . .' Sophie said.

'Do not forget,' the BFG said, 'that human beans is disappearing everywhere all the time even *without* the giants is guzzling them up. Human beans is killing each other much quicker than the giants is doing it.'

'But they don't *eat* each other,' Sophie said.

'Giants isn't eating each other either,' the BFG said. 'Nor is giants *killing* each other. Giants is not very lovely, but they is not killing each other. Nor is crockadowndillies killing other crockadowndillies. Nor is pussy-cats killing pussy-cats.'

'They kill mice,' Sophie said.

'Ah, but they is not killing their own kind,' the BFG said. 'Human beans is the only animals that is killing their own kind.'

'Don't poisonous snakes kill each other?' Sophie asked. She was searching desperately for another creature that behaved as badly as the human.

'Even poisnowse snakes is never killing each other,' the BFG said. 'Nor is the most fearsome creatures like tigers and rhinostossterisses. None of them is ever killing their own kind. Has you ever thought about that?'

Sophie kept silent.

'I is not understanding human beans at all,' the BFG said. '*You* is a human bean and you is saying it is grizzling and horrigust for giants to be eating human beans. Right or left?'

'Right,' Sophie said.

'But human beans is squishing *each other* all the time,' the BFG said. 'They is shootling guns and going up in

78

aerioplanes to drop their bombs on each other's heads every week. Human beans is always killing other human beans.'

He was right. Of course he was right and Sophie knew it. She was beginning to wonder whether humans were actually any better than giants. 'Even so,' she said, defending her own race, 'I think it's rotten that those foul giants should go off every night to eat humans. Humans have never done *them* any harm.'

'That is what the little piggy-wig is saying every day,' the BFG answered. 'He is saying, "I has never done any harm to the human bean so why should he be eating me?"'

'Oh dear,' Sophie said.

'The human beans is making rules to suit themselves,' the BFG went on. 'But the rules they is making do not suit the little piggy-wiggies. Am I right or left?'

'Right,' Sophie said.

'Giants is also making rules. Their rules is not suiting the human beans. Everybody is making his own rules to suit himself.'

'But you don't like it that those beastly giants are eating humans every night, do you?' Sophie asked.

'I do not,' the BFG answered firmly. 'One right is not making two lefts. Is you quite cosy down there in my pocket?'

'I'm fine,' Sophie said.

Then suddenly, once again, the BFG went into that magical top gear of his. He began hurtling forward with phenomenal leaps. His speed was unbelievable. The landscape became blurred and again Sophie had to duck down out of the whistling gale to save her head from being blown off her shoulders. She crouched in the pocket and listened to the wind screaming past. It came knifing in through the tiny peep-hole in the pocket and whooshed around her like a hurricane.

But this time the BFG didn't stay in top gear long. It seemed as though he had had some barrier to cross, a vast mountain perhaps or an ocean or a great desert, but having crossed it, he once again slowed down to his normal gallop and Sophie was able to pop her head up and look out once more at the view.

She noticed immediately that they were now in an altogether paler country. The sun had disappeared above a film of vapour. The air was becoming cooler every minute. The land was flat and treeless and there seemed to be no colour in it at all.

Every minute, the mist became thicker. The air became colder still and everything became paler and paler until soon there was nothing but grey and white all around them. They were in a country of swirling mists and ghostly vapours. There was some sort of grass under-foot but it was not green. It was ashy grey. There was no sign of a living creature and no sound at all except for the soft thud of the BFG's footsteps as he hurtled on through the fog.

Suddenly he stopped. 'We is here at last!' he announced. He bent down and lifted Sophie from his pocket and put her on the ground. She was still in her nightie and her feet were bare. She shivered and stared around her at the swirling mists and ghostly vapours.

'Where are we?' she asked.

'We is in Dream Country,' the BFG said. 'This is where all dreams is beginning.'

Dream-Catching

The Big Friendly Giant put the suitcase on the ground. He bent down low so that his enormous face was close to Sophie's. 'From now on, we is keeping as still as winky little micies,' he whispered.

Sophie nodded. The misty vapour swirled around her. It made her cheeks damp and left dewdrops in her hair.

The BFG opened the suitcase and took out several empty glass jars. He set them ready on the ground, with their screw tops removed. Then he stood up very straight. His head was now high up in the swirling mist and it kept disappearing, then appearing again. He was holding the long net in his right hand.

Sophie, staring upwards, saw through the mist that his colossal ears were beginning to swivel out from his head. They began waving gently to and fro.

Suddenly the BFG pounced. He leaped high in the air and swung the net through the mist with a great swishing sweep of his arm. 'Got him!' he cried. 'A jar! A jar! Quick quick quick!' Sophie picked up a jar and held it up to him. He grabbed hold of it. He lowered the net. Very carefully he tipped something absolutely invisible from the net into the jar. He dropped the net and swiftly clapped one hand over the jar. 'The top!' he whispered. 'The jar top quick!' Sophie picked up the screw top and handed it to him. He screwed it on tight and the jar was closed. The BFG was very excited. He held the jar close to one ear and listened intently.

'It's a winksquiffler!' he whispered with a thrill in his voice. 'It's ... it's ... it's ... it's even better. It's a phizz-wizard! It's a golden phizzwizard!'

Sophie stared at him.

'Oh my, oh my!' he said, holding the jar in front of him. 'This will be giving some little tottler a very happy night when I is blowing it in!'

'Is it really a good one?' Sophie asked.

'A *good one?*' he cried. 'It's a golden phizzwizard! It is not often I is getting one of these!' He handed the jar to Sophie and said, 'Please be still as a starfish now. I is thinking there may be a whole swarm of phizzwizards up here today. And do kindly stop breathing. You is terribly noisy down there.'

'I haven't moved a muscle,' Sophie said.

'Then don't,' the BFG answered sharply. Once again he stood up tall in the mist, holding his net at the ready. Then came the long silence, the waiting, the listening, and at last, with surprising suddenness came the leap and the swish of the net.

'Another jar!' he cried. 'Quick quick quick!'

When the second dream was safely in the jar and the top was screwed down, the BFG held it to his ear.

'Oh *no!*' he cried. 'Oh mince my maggots! Oh swipe my swoggles!'

'What's the matter?' Sophie asked.

'It's a trogglehumper!' he shouted. His voice was filled with fury and anguish. 'Oh, save our solos!' he cried. 'Deliver us from weasels! The devil is dancing on my dibbler!'

'What *are* you talking about?' Sophie said. The BFG was getting more distressed every moment.

'Oh, bash my eyebones!' he cried, waving the jar in the air. 'I come all this way to get lovely golden dreams and what is I catching?'

'What *are* you catching?' Sophie said.

'I is catching a frightsome trogglehumper!' he cried. 'This is a *bad bad dream!* It is worse than a bad dream! It is a *nightmare!*'

'Oh dear,' Sophie said. 'What will you do with that?'

'I is never never letting it go!' the BFG cried. 'If I do, then some poor little tottler will be having the most curdbloodling time! This one is a real kicksy bog-thumper! I is exploding it as soon as I get home!'

'Nightmares are horrible,' Sophie said. 'I had one once and I woke up sweating all over.'

'With this one you would be waking up *screaming* all over!' the BFG said. 'This one would make your teeth stand on end! If this one got into you, your blood would be freezing to icicles and your skin would go creeping across the floor!'

'Is it as bad as that?'

'It's worse!' cried the BFG. 'This is a real whoppsy grobswitcher!'

'You said it was a trogglehumper,' Sophie told him.

'It *is* a trogglehumper!' cried the exasperated BFG. 'But it is also a *bogthumper* and a *grobswitcher*! It is all three riddled into one! Oh, I is so glad I is clutching it tight. Ah, you wicked beastie, you!' he cried, holding up the jar and staring into it. 'Never more is you going to be bunkdoodling the poor little human-beaney tottlers!'

84

Sophie, who was also staring into the glass jar, cried out, 'I can see it! There's something in there!'

'Of course there is something in there,' the BFG said. 'You is looking at a frightsome trogglehumper.'

'But you told me dreams were invisible.'

'They is always invisible until they is *captured*,' the BFG told her. 'After that they is losing a little of their invisibility. We is seeing this one very clearly.'

Inside the jar Sophie could see the faint scarlet outline of something that looked like a mixture between a blob of gas and a bubble of jelly. It was moving violently, thrashing against the sides of the jar and forever changing shape.

'It's wiggling all over the place!' Sophie cried. 'It's fighting to get out! It'll bash itself to bits!'

'The nastier the dream, the angrier it is getting when it is in prison,' the BFG said. 'It is the same as with wild animals. If an animal is very fierce and you is putting it in a cage, it will make a tremendous rumpledumpus. If it is a nice animal like a cockatootloo or a fogglefrump, it will sit quietly. Dreams is exactly the same. This one is a nasty fierce bogrotting nightmare. Just look at him splashing himself against the glass!'

'It's quite frightening!' Sophie cried.

'I would be hating to get this one inside me on a darksome night,' the BFG said.

'So would I!' Sophie said.

The BFG started putting the bottles back into the suitcase.

'Is that all?' Sophie asked. 'Are we going?'

'I is so upset by this trogglehumping bogthumping grobswitcher,' the BFG said, 'that I is not wishing to go on. Dream-catching is finished for today.'

Soon Sophie was back in the waistcoat pocket and the BFG was racing home as fast as he could go. When, at last, they emerged out of the mist and came again on to the hot yellow wasteland, all the other giants were sprawled out on the ground, fast asleep.

A Trogglehumper for the Fleshlumpeater

'They is always having fifty winks before they goes scumpering off to hunt human beans in the evening,' the BFG said. He stopped for a few moments to let Sophie have a better look. 'Giants is only sleeping every then and now,' he said. 'Not nearly as much as human beans. Human beans is crazy for sleeping. Is it ever occurring to you that a human bean who is fifty is spending about *twenty* years sleeping fast?'

'I must admit that never occurred to me,' Sophie said.

'You should *allow* it to occur to you,' the BFG said. 'Imagine it please. This human bean who says he is fifty has been fast asleep for twenty years and is not even knowing where he is! Not even *doing* anything! Not even thinking!'

'It's a funny thought,' Sophie said.

'Exunckly,' the BFG said. 'So what I is trying to explain to you is that a human bean who says he is fifty is not fifty, he is only thirty.'

'What about me?' Sophie said. 'I am eight.'

'You is not eight at all,' the BFG said. 'Human bean babies and little chiddlers is spending half their time sleeping, so you is only four.'

'I'm eight,' Sophie said.

'You may *think* you is eight,' the BFG said, 'but you has only spent four years of your life with your little eyes open. You is only four and please stop higgling me. Titchy little snapperwhippers like you should not be higgling around with an old sage and onions who is hundreds of years more than you.'

'How much do giants sleep?' Sophie asked.

'They is never wasting much time snozzling,' the BFG said. 'Two or three hours is enough.'

'When do *you* sleep?' Sophie asked.

'Even less,' the BFG answered. 'I is sleeping only once in a blue baboon.'

Sophie, peeping out from her pocket, examined the nine sleeping giants. They looked even more grotesque now than when they were awake. Sprawled out across the yellow plain, they covered an area about the size of a football field. Most of them were lying on their backs with their enormous mouths wide open, and they were snoring like foghorns. The noise was awful.

Suddenly the BFG gave a jump in the air. 'By gumfrog!' he cried. 'I is just having the most whoppsy-whiffling idea!'

'What?' Sophie said.

'Wait!' he cried. 'Hold your horsefeathers! Keep your skirt on! Just you wait to see what I is going to bring about!' He galloped off fast to his cave with Sophie hanging on tight to the rim of the pocket. He rolled back the stone. He entered the cave. He was very excited. He was moving quickly. 'You stay where you is in my pocket, huggybee,' he said. 'We is doing this lovely bit of buck-swashling both together.' He laid aside the dream-catching net but hung on to the suitcase. He ran across to the other side of the cave and grabbed the long trumpet thing, the one he had been carrying when

Sophie had first seen him in the village. With the suitcase in one hand and the trumpet in the other, he dashed out of the cave.

What *is* he up to now, Sophie wondered.

'Peep your head up good,' the BFG said, 'then you will get a fine winkle of what is going on.'

When the BFG came near to the sleeping giants, he slowed his pace. He began moving softly. He crept on his toes towards the ugly brutes. They were still snoring loudly. They looked repulsive, filthy, diabolical. The BFG tip-toed around them. He went past the Gizzardgulper, the Bloodbottler, the Meatdripper, the Childchewer. Then he stopped. He had reached the Fleshlumpeater. He pointed at him, then he looked down at Sophie and gave her a big wink.

He knelt on the ground and very quietly he opened the suitcase. He took out of it the glass jar containing the terrible nightmarish trogglehumper.

At that point, Sophie guessed what was going to happen next.

Owtch, she thought. This could be rather dangerous. She crouched lower in the pocket so that only the top of her head and her eyes were showing. She wanted to be ready to duck out of sight very fast should anything go wrong.

They were about ten feet away from the Fleshlumpeater's face. The snoring-snorting noise he was making was disgusting. Every now and again a big bubble of spit formed between his two open lips and then it would burst with a splash and cover his face with saliva.

Taking infinite care, the BFG unscrewed the top of the glass jar and tipped the squiggling squirming faintly scarlet trogglehumper into the wide end of his long trumpet. He put the other end of the trumpet to his lips. He aimed the instrument directly at the Fleshlump-eater's face. He took a deep breath, puffed out his cheeks and then *whoof*! He blew!

Sophie saw a flash of pale red go darting towards the giant's face. For a split second it hovered above the face. Then it was gone. It seemed to have been sucked up the giant's nose, but it had all happened so quickly, Sophie couldn't be sure.

'We had better be skiddling away quick to where it is safe,' the BFG whispered. He trotted off for about a hundred yards, then he stopped. He crouched low to the earth. 'Now,' he said, 'we is waiting for the gun and flames to begin.'

They didn't have long to wait.

The air was suddenly pierced by the most fearful roar Sophie had ever heard, and she saw the Fleshlumpeater's body, all fifty-four feet of it, rise up off the ground and fall back again with a thump. Then it began to wriggle and twist and bounce about in the most violent fashion. It was quite frightening to watch.

'Eeeow!' roared the Fleshlumpeater. 'Ayeee! Oooow!'

'He's still asleep,' the BFG whispered. 'The terrible trogglehumping nightmare is beginning to hit him.'

'Serves him right,' Sophie said. She could feel no sympathy for this great brute who ate children as though they were sugar-lumps.

'Save us!' screamed the Fleshlumpeater, thrashing about madly. 'He is after me! He is getting me!'

The thrashing of limbs and the waving of arms became

more violent by the second. It was an awesome thing to watch such a massive creature having such mighty convulsions.

'It's Jack!' bellowed the Fleshlumpeater. 'It's the grueful gruncious Jack! Jack is after me! Jack is wackcrackling me! Jack is spikesticking me! Jack is splashplunking me! It is the terrible frightswiping Jack!' The Fleshlumpeater was writhing about over the ground like some colossal tortured snake. 'Oh, spare me, Jack!' he yelled. 'Don't hurt me, Jack!'

'Who is this Jack he's on about?' Sophie whispered.

'Jack is the only human bean all giants is frightened of,' the BFG told her. 'They is all absolutely terrified of Jack. They is all hearing that Jack is a famous giant-killer.'

'Save me!' screamed the Fleshlumpeater. 'Have mercy on this poor little giant! The beanstalk! He is coming at me with his terrible spikesticking beanstalk! Take it away! I is begging you, Jack, I is praying you not to touch me with your terrible spikesticking beanstalk!'

'Us giants,' the BFG whispered, 'is not knowing very much about this dreaded human bean called Jack. We is knowing only that he is a famous giant-killer and that he is owning something called a beanstalk. We is knowing also that the beanstalk is a fearsome thing and Jack is using it to kill giants.'

Sophie couldn't stop smiling.

'What is you griggling at?' the BFG asked her, slightly nettled.

'I'll tell you later,' Sophie said.

The awful nightmare had now gripped the great brute to such an extent that he was tying his whole body into knots. 'Do not do it, Jack!' he screeched. 'I was not eating you, Jack! I is never eating human beans! I swear I has never gobbled a single human bean in all my wholesome life!'

'Liar,' said the BFG.

Just then, one of the Fleshlumpeater's flailing fists caught the still-fast-asleep Meatdripping Giant smack in the mouth. At the same time, one of his furiously thrashing legs kicked the snoring Gizzardgulping Giant right in the guts. Both the injured giants woke up and leaped to their feet.

94

'He is swiping me right in the mouth!' yelled the Meatdripper.

'He is bungswoggling me smack in the guts!' shouted the Gizzardgulper.

The two of them rushed at the Fleshlumpeater and began pounding him with their fists and feet. The wretched Fleshlumpeater woke up with a bang. He awoke straight from one nightmare into another. He roared into battle, and in the bellowing thumping rough and tumble that followed, one sleeping giant after another either got stepped upon or kicked. Soon, all nine of them were on their feet having the most almighty free-for-all. They punched and kicked and scratched and bit and butted each other as hard as they could. Blood flowed. Noses went crunch. Teeth fell out like hailstones. The giants roared and screamed and cursed, and for many minutes the noise of battle rolled across the yellow plain.

The BFG smiled a big wide smile of absolute pleasure. 'I is loving it when they is all having a good tough and rumble,' he said.

'They'll kill each other,' Sophie said.

'Never,' the BFG answered. 'Those beasts is always bishing and walloping at one another. Soon it will be getting dusky and they will be galloping off to fill their tummies.'

'They're coarse and foul and filthy,' Sophie said. 'I hate them!'

As the BFG headed back to the cave, he said quietly, 'We certainly was putting that nightmare to good use though, wasn't we?'

'Excellent use,' Sophie said. 'Well done you.'

Dreams

The Big Friendly Giant was seated at the great table in his cave and he was doing his homework.

Sophie sat cross-legged on the table-top near by, watching him at work.

The glass jar containing the one and only good dream they had caught that day stood between them.

The BFG, with great care and patience, was printing something on a piece of paper with an enormous pencil.

'What are you writing?' Sophie asked him.

'Every dream is having its special label on the bottle,' the BFG said. 'How else could I be finding the one I am wanting in a hurry?'

'But can you really and truly tell what sort of a dream it's going to be simply by listening to it?' Sophie asked.

'I can,' the BFG said, not looking up.

'But *how*? Is it by the way it hums and buzzes?'

'You is less or more right,' the BFG said. 'Every dream in the world is making a different sort of buzzy-hum music. And these grand swashboggling ears of mine is able to read that music.'

'By music, do you mean tunes?'

'I is not meaning tunes.'

'Then what *do* you mean?'

'Human beans is having their own music, right or left?'

'Right,' Sophie said. 'Lots of music.'

'And sometimes human beans is very overcome when they is hearing wonderous music. They is getting shivers down their spindels. Right or left?'

'Right,' Sophie said.

'So the music is saying something to them. It is sending a message. I do not think the human beans is knowing what that message is, but they is loving it just the same.'

'That's about right,' Sophie said.

'But because of these jumpsquiffling ears of mine,' the BFG said, 'I is not only able to *hear* the music that dreams is making but I is *understanding* it also.'

'What do you mean *understanding* it?' Sophie said.

'I can read it,' the BFG said. 'It talks to me. It is like a langwitch.'

98

'I find that just a little hard to believe,' Sophie said.

'I'll bet you is also finding it hard to believe in quogwinkles,' the BFG said, 'and how they is visiting us from the stars.'

'Of course I don't believe that,' Sophie said.

The BFG regarded her gravely with those huge eyes of his. 'I hope you will forgive me,' he said, 'if I tell you that human beans is thinking they is very clever, but they is not. They is nearly all of them notmuchers and squeakpips.'

'I *beg* your pardon,' Sophie said.

'The matter with human beans,' the BFG went on, 'is that they is absolutely refusing to believe in anything unless they is actually seeing it right in front of their own schnozzles. Of course quogwinkles is existing. I is meeting them oftenly. I is even chittering to them.' He turned away contemptuously from Sophie and resumed his writing. Sophie moved over to read what he had written so far. The letters were printed big and bold, but were not very well formed. Here is what it said:

THIS DREAM IS ABOUT HOW I IS SAVING MY TEECHER FROM DROWNING. I IS DIVING INTO THE RIVER FROM A HIGH BRIDGE AND I IS DRAGGING MY TEECHER TO THE BANK AND THEN I IS GIVING HIM THE KISS OF DEATH . . .

'The kiss of *what?*' Sophie asked.

The BFG stopped writing and raised his head slowly. His eyes rested on Sophie's face. 'I is telling you once before,' he said quietly, 'that I is never having a chance to go to school. I is full of mistakes. They is not my fault. I do my best. You is a lovely little girl, but please remember that *you* is not exactly Miss Knoweverything yourself.'

'I'm sorry,' Sophie said. 'I really am. It is very rude of me to keep correcting you.'

The BFG gazed at her for a while longer, then he bent his head again to his slow laborious writing.

'Tell me honestly,' Sophie said. 'If you blew this dream into my bedroom when I was asleep, would I really and truly start dreaming about how I saved my teacher from drowning by diving off the bridge?'

'More,' the BFG said. 'A lot more. But I cannot be squibbling the whole gropefluncking dream on a titchy bit of paper. Of course there is more.'

The BFG laid down his pencil and placed one massive ear close to the jar. For about thirty seconds he listened intently. 'Yes,' he said, nodding his great head solemnly up and down. 'This dream is continuing very nice. It has a very dory-hunky ending.'

'How does it end?' Sophie said. '*Please* tell me.'

'You would be dreaming,' the BFG said, 'that the morning after you is saving the teacher from the river, you is arriving at school and you is seeing all the five hundred pupils sitting in the assembly hall, and all the teachers as well, and the head teacher is then standing up and saying, "I is wanting the whole school to give three cheers for Sophie because she is so brave and is saving the life of our fine arithmatic teacher, Mr Figgins, who was unfortunately pushed off the bridge into the river by our gym-teacher, Miss Amelia Upscotch. So three cheers for Sophie!" And the whole school is then cheering like mad and shouting bravo well done, and, for ever after that, even when you is getting your sums all gungswizzled and muggled up, Mr Figgins is always giving you ten out of ten and writing *Good Work Sophie* in your exercise book. Then you is waking up.'

'I like that dream,' Sophie said.

'Of course you like it,' the BFG said. 'It is a phizz-wizard.' He licked the back of the label and stuck it on the jar. 'I is usually writing a bit more than this on the labels,' he said. 'But you is watching me and making me jumpsy.'

'I'll go and sit somewhere else,' Sophie said.

'Don't go,' he said. 'Look in the jar carefully and I think you will be seeing this dream.'

Sophie peered into the jar and there, sure enough, she saw the faint translucent outline of something about the size of a hen's egg. There was just a touch of colour in it, a pale sea-green, soft and shimmering and very beautiful. There it lay, this small oblong sea-green jellyish thing, at the bottom of the jar, quite peaceful, but pulsing gently, the whole of it moving in and out ever so slightly, as though it were breathing.

'It's moving!' Sophie cried. 'It's alive!'

'Of course it's alive.'

'What will you feed it on?' Sophie asked.

'It is not needing any food,' the BFG told her.

'That's cruel,' Sophie said. 'Everything alive needs food of some sort. Even trees and plants.'

'The north wind is alive,' the BFG said. 'It is moving. It touches you on the cheek and on the hands. But nobody is feeding it.'

Sophie was silent. This extraordinary giant was disturbing her ideas. He seemed to be leading her towards mysteries that were beyond her understanding.

'A dream is not needing anything,' the BFG went on. 'If it is a good one, it is waiting peaceably for ever until it is released and allowed to do its job. If it is a bad one, it is always fighting to get out.'

The BFG stood up and walked over to one of the many shelves and placed the latest jar among the thousands of others.

'Please can I see some of the other dreams?' Sophie asked him.

The BFG hesitated. 'Nobody is ever seeing them before,' he said. 'But perhaps after all I is letting you have a little peep.' He picked her up off the table and stood her on the palm of one of his huge hands. He carried her towards the shelves. 'Over here is some of the good dreams,' he said. 'The phizzwizards.'

'Would you hold me closer so I can read the labels,' Sophie said.

'My labels is only telling bits of it,' the BFG said. 'The dreams is usually much longer. The labels is just to remind me.'

Sophie started to read the labels. The first one seemed long enough to her. It went right round the jar, and as she read it, she had to keep turning the jar. This is what it said:

TODAY I IS SITTING IN CLASS AND I DISCOVER
THAT IF I IS STARING VERY HARD AT MY TEECHER
IN A SPHESHAL WAY, I IS ABLE TO PUT HER TO
SLEEP. SO I KEEP STARING AT HER AND IN THE END
HER HEAD DROPS ON TO HER DESK AND SHE GOES
FAST TO SLEEP AND SNORKLES LOUDLY. THEN IN
MARCHES THE HEAD TEACHER AND HE SHOUTS
'WAKE UP MISS PLUMRIDGE! HOW DARE YOU GO
TO SLEEP IN CLASS! GO FETCH YOUR HAT AND COTE
AND LEAVE THIS SCHOOL FOR EVER! YOU IS
SACKED!' BUT IN A JIFFY I IS PUTTING THE HEAD
TEECHER TO SLEEP AS WELL, AND HE JUST
CRUMPLES SLOWLY TO THE FLOOR LIKE A LUMP OF
JELLY AND THERE HE LIES ALL IN A HEAP AND
STARTS SNORKELLING EVEN LOWDER THAN MISS
PLUMRIDGE. AND THEN I IS HEARING MY MUMMY'S
VOICE SAYING WAKE UP YOUR BREKFUST IS
REDDY.

'What a funny dream,' Sophie said.

'It's a ringbeller,' the BFG said. 'It's whoppsy.'

Inside the jar, just below the edge of the label, Sophie
could see the putting-to-sleep dream lying peacefully on
the bottom, pulsing gently, sea-green like the other one,
but perhaps a trifle larger.

'Do you have separate dreams for boys and for girls?'
Sophie asked.

'Of course,' the BFG said. 'If I is giving a girl's dream to a boy, even if it was a really whoppsy girl's dream, the boy would be waking up and thinking what a rotbungling grinksludging old dream that was.'

'Boys would,' Sophie said.

'These here is all girls' dreams on this shelf,' the BFG said.

'Can I read a boy's dream?'

'You can,' the BFG said, and he lifted her to a higher shelf. The label on the nearest boy's-dream jar read as follows:

I IS MAKING MYSELF A MARVELUS PAIR OF SUCTION BOOTS AND WHEN I PUT THEM ON I IS ABEL TO WALK STRATE UP THE KITSHUN WALL AND ACROSS THE CEILING. WELL, I IS WALKING UPSIDE DOWN ON THE CEILING WEN MY BIG SISTER COMES IN AND SHE IS STARTING TO YELL AT ME AS SHE

ALWAYS DOES, YELLING WOT ON EARTH IS YOU
DOING UP THERE WALKING ON THE CEILING AND I
LOOKS DOWN AT HER AND I SMILES AND I SAYS I
TOLD YOU YOU WAS DRIVING ME UP THE WALL AND
NOW YOU HAS DONE IT.

'I find that one rather silly,' Sophie said.
'Boys wouldn't,' the BFG said, grinning. 'It's another ringbeller. Perhaps you has seen enough now.'
'Let me read another boy's one,' Sophie said.
The next label said:

THE TELLYFONE RINGS IN OUR HOUSE AND MY
FATHER PICKS IT UP AND SAYS IN HIS VERY
IMPORTANT TELLYFONE VOICE 'SIMPKINS
SPEAKING'. THEN HIS FACE GOES WHITE AND HIS
VOICE GOES ALL FUNNY AND HE SAYS '*WHAT!*
WHO?' AND THEN HE SAYS 'YES SIR I UNDERSTAND
SIR BUT SURELY IT IS *ME* YOU IS WISHING TO SPEKE
TO SIR NOT MY LITTLE SON?' MY FATHER'S FACE IS
GOING FROM WHITE TO DARK PURPLE AND HE IS
GULPING LIKE HE HAS A LOBSTER STUCK IN HIS
THROTE AND THEN AT LAST HE IS SAYING 'YES SIR
VERY WELL SIR I WILL GET HIM SIR' AND HE TURNS
TO ME AND HE SAYS IN A RATHER RESPECKFUL
VOICE 'IS YOU KNOWING THE PRESIDENT OF THE
UNITED STATES?' AND I SAYS 'NO BUT I EXPECT HE
IS HEARING ABOUT ME.' THEN I IS HAVING A LONG
TALK ON THE FONE AND SAYING THINGS LIKE 'LET
ME TAKE CARE OF IT, MR PRESIDENT. YOU'LL
BUNGLE IT ALL UP IF YOU DO IT YOUR WAY'. AND MY
FATHER'S EYES IS GOGGLING RIGHT OUT OF HIS

HEAD AND THAT IS WHEN I IS HEARING MY
FATHER'S REAL VOICE SAYING GET UP YOU LAZY
SLOB OR YOU WILL BE LATE FOR SKOOL.

'Boys are crazy,' Sophie said. 'Let me read this next
one.' Sophie started reading the next label:

I IS HAVING A BATH AND I IS DISCOVERING THAT
IF I PRESS QUITE HARD ON MY TUMMY BUTTON A
FUNNY FEELING COMES OVER ME AND SUDDENLEY
MY LEGS IS NOT THERE NOR IS MY ARMS. IN FACT I
HAS BECOME ABSOLOOTLY INVISIBLE ALL OVER. I
IS STILL THERE BUT NO ONE CAN SEE ME NOT EVEN
MYSELF. SO MY MUMMY COMES IN AND SAYS 'WHERE
IS THAT CHILD! HE WAS IN THE BATH A MINIT AGO
AND HE CAN'T POSSIBLY HAVE WASHED HIMSELF
PROPERLY!' SO I SAYS 'HERE I IS' AND SHE SAYS
'WHERE?' AND I SAYS 'HERE' AND SHE SAYS
'WHERE?' AND I SAYS 'HERE!' AND SHE YELLS
'HENRY! COME UP QUICK!' AND WHEN MY DADDY
RUSHES IN I IS WASHING MYSELF AND MY DADDY

SEES THE SOAP FLOATING AROUND IN THE AIR BUT OF CORSE HE IS NOT SEEING ME AND HE SHOUTS 'WHERE ARE YOU BOY?' AND I SAYS 'HERE' AND HE SAYS 'WHERE?' AND I SAYS 'HERE' AND HE SAYS '*WHERE?*' AND I SAYS '*HERE!*' AND HE SAYS 'THE SOAP, BOY! THE SOAP! IT'S FLYING IN THE AIR!' THEN I PRESS MY TUMMY BUTTON AGAIN AND NOW I IS VISIBLE. MY DADDY IS SQUIFFY WITH EX-CITEMENT AND HE SAYS 'YOU IS THE INVISIBLE BOY!' AND I SAYS 'NOW I IS GOING TO HAVE SOME FUN,' SO WHEN I IS OUT OF THE BATH AND I HAVE DRIED MYSELF I PUT ON MY DRESSING-GOWN AND SLIPPERS AND I PRESS MY TUMMY BUTTON AGAIN TO BECOME INVISIBLE AND I GO DOWN INTO THE TOWN AND WALK IN THE STREETS. OF CORSE ONLY ME IS INVISIBLE BUT NOT THE THINGS I IS WEARING SO WHEN PEEPLE IS SEEING A DRESSING GOWN AND SLIPPERS FLOATING ALONG THE STREET WITH NOBODY IN IT THERE IS A PANIC WITH EVERYBODY YELLING 'A GHOST! A GHOST!' AND PEEPLE IS SCREAMING LEFT AND RIGHT AND BIG STRONG POLICEMEN IS RUNNING FOR THEIR LIVES AND BEST OF ALL I SEE MR GRUMMIT MY ALGEBRA

TEECHER COMING OUT OF A PUB AND I FLOAT UP TO HIM AND SAY 'BOO!' AND HE LETS OUT A FRIGHTSOME HOWL AND DASHES BACK INTO THE PUB AND THEN I IS WAKING UP AND FEELING HAPPY AS A WHIFFSQUIDDLER.

'Pretty ridiculous,' Sophie said. All the same, she couldn't resist reaching down and pressing her own tummy button to see if it worked. Nothing happened.

'Dreams is very mystical things,' the BFG said. 'Human beans is not understanding them at all. Not even their brainiest prossefors is understanding them. Has you seen enough?'

'Just this last one,' Sophie said. 'This one here.'

She started reading:

I HAS RITTEN A BOOK AND IT IS SO EXCITING NOBODY CAN PUT IT DOWN. AS SOON AS YOU HAS RED THE FIRST LINE YOU IS SO HOOKED ON IT YOU CANNOT STOP UNTIL THE LAST PAGE. IN ALL THE CITIES PEEPLE IS WALKING IN THE STREETS BUMPING INTO EACH OTHER BECAUSE THEIR FACES IS BURIED IN MY BOOK AND DENTISTS IS READING IT AND TRYING TO FILL TEETHS AT THE SAME TIME BUT NOBODY MINDS BECAUSE THEY IS ALL READING IT TOO IN THE DENTIST'S CHAIR. DRIVERS IS READING IT WHILE DRIVING AND CARS IS CRASHING ALL OVER THE COUNTRY. BRAIN SURGEONS IS READING IT WHILE THEY IS OPERATING ON BRAINS AND AIRLINE PILOTS IS READING IT AND GOING TO TIMBUCTOO INSTEAD OF LONDON. FOOTBALL PLAYERS IS READING IT ON

THE FIELD BECAUSE THEY CAN'T PUT IT DOWN
AND SO IS OLIMPICK RUNNERS WHILE THEY IS
RUNNING. EVERYBODY HAS TO SEE WHAT IS GOING
TO HAPPEN NEXT IN MY BOOK AND WHEN I WAKE
UP I IS STILL TINGLING WITH EXCITEMENT AT
BEING THE GREATEST RITER THE WORLD HAS
EVER KNOWN UNTIL MY MUMMY COMES IN AND SAYS
I WAS LOOKING AT YOUR ENGLISH EXERCISE BOOK
LAST NITE AND REALLY YOUR SPELLING IS
ATROSHUS SO IS YOUR PUNTULASHON.

'That's enough for now,' the BFG said. 'There is
dillions more but my arm is getting tired holding you up.'

'What are all those over there?' Sophie said. 'Why
have they got such tiny labels?'

'That,' the BFG said, 'is because one day I is catching
so many dreams I is not having the time or energy to
write out long labels. But there is enough to remind me.'

'Can I look?' Sophie said.

The long-suffering BFG carried her across to the jars she was pointing to. Sophie read them rapidly, one after the other:

I IS CLIMBING MOUNT EVERAST WITH JUST MY PUSSY-CAT FOR CUMPANY.

I IS INVENTING A CAR THAT RUNS ON TOOTH-PASTE.

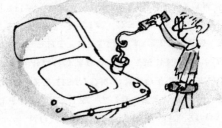

I IS ABLE TO MAKE THE ELEKTRIK LITES GO ON AND OFF JUST BY WISHING IT.

I IS ONLY AN EIGHT YEAR OLD LITTLE BOY BUT
I IS GROWING A SPLENDID BUSHY BEARD AND ALL
THE OTHER BOYS IS JALOUS.

I IS ABEL TO JUMP OUT OF ANY HIGH WINDOW
AND FLOTE DOWN SAFELY.

I HAS A PET BEE THAT MAKES ROCK AND ROLL
MUSIK WHEN IT FLIES.

'What amazes me,' Sophie said, 'is how you ever learned to write in the first place.'

'Ah,' said the BFG. 'I has been wondering how long it is before you is asking me that.'

'Considering you never went to school, I think it's quite marvellous,' Sophie said. 'How *did* you learn?'

The BFG crossed the cave and opened a tiny secret door in the wall. He took out a book, very old and tattered. By human standards, it was an ordinary sized book, but it looked like a postage stamp in his huge hand.

'One night,' he said, 'I is blowing a dream through a window and I sees this book lying on the little boy's bedroom table. I wanted it so very badly, you understand. But I is refusing to steal it. I would never do that.'

'So how did you get it?' Sophie asked.

'I *borrowed* it,' the BFG said, smiling a little. 'Just for a short time I borrowed it.'

'How long have you had it?' Sophie asked.

'Perhaps only about eighty years,' the BFG said. 'Soon I shall be putting it back.'

'And that's how you taught yourself to write?' Sophie asked him.

'I is reading it hundreds of times,' the BFG said. 'And I is still reading it and teaching new words to myself and

how to write them. It is the most scrumdiddlyumptious story.'

Sophie took the book out of his hand. '*Nicholas Nickleby*,' she read aloud.

'By Dahl's Chickens,' the BFG said.

'By *who?*' Sophie said.

Just then, there came a tremendous noise of galloping feet from outside the cave. 'What's that?' Sophie cried.

'That is all the giants zippfizzing off to another country to guzzle human beans,' the BFG said. He quickly popped Sophie into his waistcoat pocket, then hurried to the cave entrance and rolled back the stone.

Sophie, peeping out of her spy-hole, saw all nine of the fearsome giants coming past at full gallop.

'Where is you off to tonight?' shouted the BFG.

'We is all of us flushbunking off to England tonight,' answered the Fleshlumpeater as they went galloping past. 'England is a luctuous land and we is fancying a few nice little English chiddlers.'

'I,' shouted the Maidmasher, 'is knowing where there is a gigglehouse for girls and I is guzzling myself full as a frothblower!'

'And I knows where there is a bogglebox for boys!' shouted the Gizzardgulper. 'All I has to do is reach in and grab myself a handful! English boys is tasting extra lickswishy!'

In a few seconds, the nine galloping giants were out of sight.

'What *did* he mean?' Sophie said, poking her head out of the pocket. 'What is a gigglehouse for girls?'

'He is meaning a girls' school,' the BFG said. 'He will be eating them by the bundle.'

'Oh no!' cried Sophie.

'And boys from a boys' school,' said the BFG.

'It mustn't happen!' Sophie cried out. 'We've got to stop them! We can't just sit here and do nothing!'

'There's not a thing we can do,' the BFG said. 'We is helpless as horsefeathers.' He sat down on a large craggy blue rock near the entrance to his cave. He took Sophie from his pocket and put her beside him on the rock. 'It is now quite safe for you to be outside until they is coming back,' he said.

The sun had dipped below the horizon and it was getting dark.

The Great Plan

'We've absolutely *got* to stop them!' Sophie cried. 'Put me back in your pocket quick and we'll chase after them and warn everyone in England they're coming.'

'Redunculus and *um*-possible,' the BFG said. 'They is going two times as fast as me and they is finishing their guzzle before we is halfway.'

'But we can't just sit here doing nothing!' Sophie cried. 'How many girls and boys are they going to eat tonight?'

'Many,' the BFG said. 'The Fleshlumpeating Giant alone has a most squackling whoppsy appetite.'

'Will he snatch them out of their beds while they're sleeping?'

'Like peas out of a poddle,' the BFG said.

'I can't bear to think of it!' Sophie cried.

'Then don't,' the BFG said. 'For years and years I is sitting here on this very rock every night after night when they is galloping away, and I is feeling so sad for all the human beans they is going to gobble up. But I has had to get used to it. There is nothing I can do. If I wasn't a titchy little runty giant only twenty-four feet high then I would be stopping them. But that is absolutely out of the window.'

'Do you always know where they're going?' Sophie asked.

'Always,' the BFG said. 'Every night they is yelling at

me as they go bootling past. The other day they was yelling "We is off to Mrs Sippi and Miss Souri to guzzle them both!"'

'Disgusting,' Sophie said. 'I hate them.'

She and the Big Friendly Giant sat quietly side by side on the blue rock in the gathering dusk. Sophie had never felt so helpless in her life. After a while, she stood up and cried out, 'I can't stand it! Just think of those poor girls and boys who are going to be eaten alive in a few hours time! We can't just sit here and do nothing! We've got to go after those brutes!'

'No,' the BFG said.

'We must!' Sophie cried. 'Why won't you go?'

The BFG sighed and shook his head firmly. 'I has told you five or six times,' he said, 'and the third will be the last. I is *never* showing myself to human beans.'

'Why ever not?'

'If I do, they will be putting me in the zoo with all the jiggyraffes and cattypiddlers.'

'Nonsense,' Sophie said.

'And they will be sending *you* straight back to a norphanage,' the BFG went on. 'Grown-up human beans is not famous for their kindnesses. They is all squifflerotters and grinksludgers.'

'That simply isn't true!' Sophie cried angrily. 'Some of them are very kind indeed.'

'Who?' the BFG said. 'Name one.'

'The Queen of England,' Sophie said. 'You can't call her a squifflerotter or a grinksludger.'

'Well ...' the BFG said.

'You can't call her a squeakpip or a notmucher either,' Sophie said, getting angrier and angrier.

'The Fleshlumpeater is longing dearly to guzzle her up,' the BFG said, smiling a little now.

'Who, the *Queen*?' Sophie cried, aghast.

'Yes,' the BFG answered. 'Fleshlumpeater says he is never eating a queen and he thinks perhaps she has an especially scrumdiddlyumptious flavour.'

'How dare he!' Sophie cried.

'But Fleshlumpeater says there is too many soldiers around her palace and he dursent try it.'

'He'd better not!' Sophie said.

'He is also saying he would like very much to guzzle one of the soldiers in his pretty red suit but he is worried about those big black furry hats they is wearing. He thinks they might be sticking in his throat.'

'I hope he chokes,' Sophie said.

'Fleshlumpeater is a very careful giant,' the BFG said.

Sophie was silent for a few moments. Then suddenly, in a voice filled with excitement, she cried out, 'I've got it! By golly, I think I've got it!'

'Got what?' asked the BFG.

'The answer!' cried Sophie. 'We'll go to the Queen! It's a terrific idea! If I went and told the Queen about these disgusting man-eating giants, I'm sure she'd do something about it!'

The BFG looked down at her sadly and shook his head. 'She is never believing you,' he said. 'Never in a month of Mondays.'

'I think she would.'

'Never,' the BFG said. 'It is sounding such a wonky tall story, the Queen will be laughing and saying "What awful rubbsquash!"'

'She would not!'

'Of course she would,' the BFG said. 'I has told you before that human beans is simply not *believing* in giants.'

'Then it's up to us to find a way of *making* her believe in them,' Sophie said.

'And how is you getting in to see the Queen anyway?' the BFG asked.

'Now hold on a sec,' Sophie said. 'Just you hold on a sec because I've got another idea.'

'Your ideas is full of crodswoggle,' the BFG said.

'Not this one,' Sophie said. 'You say that if we tell the Queen, she would never believe us?'

'I is certain she wouldn't,' the BFG said.

'But we aren't *going* to tell her!' Sophie said excitedly. 'We don't *have* to tell her! We'll make her *dream* it!'

'That is an even more frothbungling suggestion,' the BFG said. 'Dreams is lots of fun but nobody is believing in dreams either. You is only believing in a dream while you is actually dreaming it. But as soon as you is waking up you is saying "Oh thank goodness it was only a dream".'

'Don't you worry about that part of it,' Sophie said. 'I can fix that.'

'Never can you fix it,' the BFG said.

'I can! I swear I can! But first of all, let me ask you a very important question. Here it is. Can you make a person dream absolutely anything in the world?'

'Anything you like,' the BFG said proudly.

'If I said I wanted to dream that I was in a flying bathtub with silver wings, could you make me dream it?'

'I could,' the BFG said.

'But how?' Sophie said. 'You obviously don't have exactly that dream in your collection.'

'I do not,' the BFG said. 'But I could soon be mixing it up.'

'How could you mix it up?'

'It is a little bit like mixing a cake,' the BFG said. 'If you is putting the right amounts of all the different things into it, you is making the cake come out any way you want, sugary, splongy, curranty, Christmassy or grobswitchy. It is the same with dreams.'

'Go on,' Sophie said.

'I has dillions of dreams on my shelfs, right or left?'

'Right,' Sophie said.

'I has dreams about bathtubs, lots of them. I has dreams about silver wings. I has dreams about flying. So all I has to do is mix those dreams together in the proper way and I is very quickly making a dream where you is flying in a bathtub with silver wings.'

'I see what you mean,' Sophie said. 'But I didn't know you could mix one dream with another.'

'Dreams *like* being mixed,' the BFG answered. 'They is getting very lonesome all by themselves in those glassy bottles.'

'Right,' Sophie said. 'Now then, do you have dreams about the Queen of England?'

'Lots of them,' the BFG said.

'And about giants?'

'Of course,' the BFG said.

'And about giants eating people?'

'Swiggles of them,' the BFG said.

'And about little girls like me?'

'Those is commonest of all,' the BFG said. 'I has bottles and bottles of dreams about little girls.'

'And you could mix them all up just as I want you to?' Sophie asked, getting more and more excited.

'Of course,' the BFG said. 'But how is this helping us? I think you is barking up the wrong dog.'

'Now hold on,' Sophie said. 'Listen carefully. I want you to mix a dream which you will blow into the Queen of England's bedroom when she is asleep. And this is how it will go.'

'Now hang on a mintick,' the BFG said. 'How is I possibly going to get near enough to the Queen of

England's bedroom to blow in my dream? You is talking dumbsilly.'

'I'll tell you that later,' Sophie said. 'For the moment please listen carefully. Here is the dream I want you to mix. Are you paying attention?'

'Very close,' the BFG said.

'I want the Queen to dream that nine disgusting giants, each one about fifty feet tall, are galloping to England in the night. She must dream their names as well. What are their names again?'

'Fleshlumpeater,' the BFG said. 'Manhugger. Bonecruncher. Childchewer. Meatdripper. Gizzardgulper. Maidmasher. Bloodbottler. And the Butcher Boy.'

'Let her dream all those names,' Sophie said. 'And let her dream that they will be creeping into England in the depths of the witching hour and snatching little boys and girls from their beds. Let her dream that they will be reaching into the bedroom windows and pulling the little boys and girls out of their beds and then ...' Sophie paused. 'Do they eat them on the spot or do they carry them away first?' she asked.

'They is usually just popping them straight into their mouths like popcorn,' the BFG said.

'Put that in the dream,' Sophie said. 'And then ... then the dream must say that when their tummies are full, they will go galloping back to Giant Country where no one can find them.'

'Is that all?' the BFG said.

'Certainly not,' Sophie said. 'You must then explain to the Queen in her dream that there is a Big Friendly Giant who can tell her where all those beasts are living, so that she can send her soldiers and her armies to capture them once and for all. And now let her dream one last and very important thing. Let her dream that there is a little girl called Sophie sitting on her window-sill who will tell her where the Big Friendly Giant is hiding.'

'Where is he hiding?' asked the BFG.

'We'll come to that later,' Sophie said. 'So the Queen dreams her dream, right?'

'Right,' the BFG said.

'Then she wakes up and the first thing she thinks is oh what a horrid dream. I'm so glad it *was* only a dream. And then she looks up from her pillow and what does she see?'

'What *does* she see?' the BFG asked.

'She sees a little girl called Sophie sitting on her window-sill, right there in real life before her very eyes.'

'How is you going to be sitting on the Queen's window-sill, may I beg?' the BFG said.

'*You* are going to put me there,' Sophie said. 'And that's the lovely part about it. If someone *dreams* that there is a little girl sitting on her window-sill and then she wakes up and sees that the little girl *really is* sitting there, that is a dream come true, is it not?'

'I is beginning to see where you is driving to,' the BFG said. 'If the Queen is knowing that part of her dream is true, then perhaps she is believing the rest of it is true as well.'

'That's about it,' Sophie said. 'But I shall have to convince her of that myself.'

'You said you is wanting the dream to say there is a Big Friendly Giant who is also going to talk to the Queen?'

'Absolutely,' Sophie said. 'You must. You are the only one who can tell her where to find the other giants.'

'How is I meeting the Queen?' asked the BFG. 'I is not wanting to be shooted at by her soldiers.'

'The soldiers are only in the front of the Palace,' Sophie said. 'At the back there is a huge garden and there are no soldiers in there at all. There is a very high wall with spikes on it around the garden to stop people climbing in. But you could simply walk over that.'

'How is you knowing all this about the Queen's Palace?' the BFG asked.

'Last year I was in a different orphanage,' Sophie said. 'It was in London and we used to go for walks all around there.'

'Is you helping me to find this Palace?' the BFG asked. 'I has never dared to go hide and sneaking around London in my life.'

'I'll show you the way,' Sophie said confidently.

'I is frightened of London,' the BFG said.

'Don't be,' Sophie said. 'It's full of tiny dark streets and there are very few people about in the witching hour.'

The BFG picked Sophie up between one finger and a thumb and placed her gently in the palm of the other hand. 'Is the Queen's Palace very big?' he asked.

'Huge,' Sophie said.

'Then how is we finding the right bedroom?'

'That's up to you,' Sophie said. 'You're supposed to be an expert at that sort of thing.'

'And you is absolutely sure the Queen will not put me in a zoo with all the cattypiddlers?'

'Of course she won't,' Sophie said. 'You'll be a hero. And you'll never have to eat snozzcumbers again.'

Sophie saw the BFG's eyes widen. He licked his lips.

'You mean it?' he said. 'You really mean it? No more disgustive snozzcumbers?'

'You couldn't get one if you wanted to,' Sophie said. 'Humans don't grow them.'

That did it. The BFG got to his feet. 'When is you wanting me to mix this special dream?' he asked.

'Now,' Sophie said. 'At once.'

'When is we going to see the Queen?' he said.

'Tonight,' Sophie said. 'As soon as you've mixed the dream.'

'Tonight?' the BFG cried. 'Why such a flushbunking flurry?'

'If we can't save tonight's children, we can anyway save tomorrow's,' Sophie said. 'What is more, I'm getting famished. I haven't had a thing to eat for twenty-four hours.'

'Then we had better get crackling,' the BFG said, moving back towards the cave.

Sophie kissed him on the tip of his thumb. 'I knew you'd do it!' she said. 'Come on! Let's hurry!'

Mixing the Dream

It was dark now. The night had already begun. The BFG, with Sophie sitting on his hand, hurried into the cave and put on those brilliant blinding lights that seemed to come from nowhere. He placed Sophie on the table. 'Stay there please,' he said, 'and no chittering. I is needing to listen only to silence when I is mixing up such a knotty plexicated dream as this.'

He hurried away from her. He got out an enormous empty glass jar that was the size of a washing machine. He clutched it to his chest and hurried towards the shelves on which stood the thousands and thousands of smaller jars containing the captured dreams.

'Dreams about giants,' he muttered to himself as he searched the labels. 'The giants is guzzling human beans ... no, not that one ... nor that one ... here's one! ... And here's another! ...' He grabbed the jars and unscrewed the tops. He tipped the dreams into the enormous jar he was clutching and as each one went in, Sophie caught a glimpse of a small sea-green blob tumbling from one jar into the other.

The BFG hurried towards another shelf. 'Now,' he muttered, 'I is wanting dreams about gigglehouses for girls ... and about boggleboxes for boys.' He was becoming very tense now. Sophie could almost see the excitement bubbling inside him as he scurried back and forth

among his beloved jars. There must have been fifty thousand dreams altogether up there on the shelves, but he seemed to know almost exactly where every one of them was. 'Dreams about a little girl,' he muttered. 'And dreams about me ... about the B F G ... come on, come on, hurry up, get on with it ... now where in the wonky world is I keeping those? ...'

And so it went on. In about half an hour the BFG had found all the dreams he wanted and had tipped them into the one huge jar. He put the jar on the table. Sophie sat watching him but said nothing. Inside the big jar, lying on the bottom of it, she could clearly see about fifty of those oval sea-green jellyish shapes, all pulsing gently in and out, some lying on top of others, but each one still a quite separate individual dream.

'Now we is mixing them,' the BFG announced. He went to the cupboard where he kept his bottles of frobscottle, and from it he took out a gigantic egg-beater. It was one of those that has a handle which you turn, and down below there are a lot of overlapping blades that go whizzing round. He inserted the bottom end of this contraption into the big jar where the dreams were lying. 'Watch,' he said. He started turning the handle very fast.

Flashes of green and blue exploded inside the jar. The dreams were being whisked into a sea-green froth.

'The poor things!' Sophie cried.

'They is not feeling it,' the BFG said as he turned the handle. 'Dreams is not like human beans or animals. They has no brains. They is made of zozimus.'

After about a minute, the BFG stopped whisking. The whole bottle was now full to the brim with large bubbles. They were almost exactly like the bubbles we ourselves blow from soapy water, except that these had even brighter and more beautiful colours swimming on their surfaces.

'Keep watching,' the BFG said.

Quite slowly, the topmost bubble rose up through the neck of the jar and floated away. A second one followed. Then a third and a fourth. Soon the cave was filled with hundreds of beautifully coloured bubbles, all drifting gently through the air. It was truly a wonderful sight. As Sophie watched them, they all started floating towards the cave entrance, which was still open.

'They're going out,' Sophie whispered.

'Of course,' the BFG said.

'Where to?'

'Those is all little tiny dream-bits that I isn't using,' the BFG said. 'They is going back to the misty country to join up with proper dreams.'

'It's all a bit beyond me,' Sophie said.

'Dreams is full of mystery and magic,' the BFG said. 'Do not try to understand them. Look in the big bottle and you will now see the dream you is wanting for the Queen.'

Sophie turned and stared into the great jar. On the

bottom of it, something was thrashing around wildly, bouncing up and down and flinging itself against the walls of the jar. 'Good heavens!' she cried. 'Is that it?'

'That's it,' the BFG said proudly.

'But it's . . . it's horrible!' Sophie cried. 'It's jumping about! It wants to get out!'

'That's because it's a trogglehumper,' the BFG said. 'It's a nightmare.'

'Oh, but I don't want you to give the Queen a nightmare!' Sophie cried.

'If she is dreaming about giants guzzling up little boys and girls, then what is you expecting it to be except a nightmare?' the BFG said.

'Oh, no!' Sophie cried.

'Oh, yes,' the BFG said. 'A dream where you is seeing little chiddlers being eaten is about the most frightsome trogglehumping dream you can get. It's a kicksy bog-thumper. It's a whoppsy grobswitcher. It is all of them riddled into one. It is as bad as that dream I blew into the Fleshlumpeater this afternoon. It is worse.'

Sophie stared down at the fearful nightmare dream that was still thrashing away in the huge glass jar. It was much larger than the others. It was about the size and shape of, shall we say, a turkey's egg. It was jellyish. It had tinges of bright scarlet deep inside it. There was

something terrible about the way it was throwing itself against the sides of the jar.

'I don't want to give the Queen a nightmare,' Sophie said.

'I is thinking,' the BFG said, 'that your Queen will be happy to have a nightmare if having a nightmare is going to save a lot of human beans from being gobbled up by filthsome giants. Is I right or is I left?'

'I suppose you're right,' Sophie said. 'It's got to be done.'

'She will soon be getting over it,' the BFG said.

'Have you put all the other important things into it?' Sophie asked.

'When I is blowing that dream into the Queen's bedroom,' the BFG said, 'she will be dreaming every single little thingalingaling you is asking me to make her dream.'

'About me sitting on the window-sill?'

'That part is very strong.'

'And about a Big Friendly Giant?'

'I is putting in a nice long gobbit about him,' the BFG said. As he spoke, he picked up one of his smaller jars and very quickly tipped the struggling thrashing troggle-humper out of the large jar into the small one. Then he screwed the lid tightly on to the small jar.

'That's it,' he announced. 'We is now ready.' He fetched his suitcase and put the small jar into it.

'Why bother to take a great big suitcase when you've only got one jar?' Sophie said. 'You could put the jar in your pocket.'

The BFG looked down at her and smiled. 'By goggles,' he said, taking the jar out of the suitcase, 'your head is not quite so full of grimesludge after all! I can see you is not born last week.'

'Thank you, kind sir,' Sophie said, making a little curtsey from the table-top.

'Is you ready to leave?' the BFG asked.

'I'm ready!' Sophie cried. Her heart was beginning to thump at the thought of what they were about to do. It really was a wild and crazy thing. Perhaps they would both be thrown into prison.

The BFG was putting on his great black cloak.

He tucked the jar into a pocket in his cloak. He picked up his long trumpet-like dream-blower. Then he turned and looked at Sophie who was still on the table-top. 'The dream-bottle is in my pocket,' he said. 'Is you going to sit in there with it during the travel?'

'Never!' cried Sophie. 'I refuse to sit next to that beastly thing!'

'Then where is you going to sit?' the BFG asked her.

Sophie looked him over for a few moments. Then she said, 'If you would be kind enough to swivel one of your lovely big ears so that it is lying flat like a dish, that would make a very cosy place for me to sit.'

'By gumbo, that is a squackling good idea!' the BFG said.

Slowly, he swivelled his huge right ear until it was like a great shell facing the heavens. He lifted Sophie up and placed her into it. The ear itself, which was about the size of a large tea-tray, was full of the same channels and crinkles as a human ear. It was extremely comfortable.

'I hope I don't fall down your earhole,' Sophie said, edging away from the large hole just beside her.

'Be very careful not to do that,' the BFG said. 'You would be giving me a cronking earache.'

The nice thing about being there was that she could whisper directly into his ear.

'You is tickling me a bit,' the BFG said. 'Please do not jiggle about.'

'I'll try not to,' Sophie said. 'Are we ready?'

'Oweeee!' yelled the BFG. 'Don't *do* that!'

'I didn't do anything,' Sophie said.

'You is talking too *loud!* You is forgetting that I is hearing every little thingalingaling fifty times louder than usual and there you is shouting away right inside my ear!'

'Oh gosh,' Sophie murmured. 'I forgot that.'

'Your voice is sounding like tunder and thrumpets!'

'I'm so sorry,' Sophie whispered. 'Is that better?'

'No!' cried the BFG. 'It sounds as though you is shoot-ling off a bunderbluss!'

'Then how can I talk to you?' Sophie whispered.

'Don't!' cried the poor BFG. 'Please don't! Each word is like you is dropping buzzbombs in my earhole!'

Sophie tried speaking right under her breath. 'Is this better?' she said. She spoke so softly she couldn't even hear her own voice.

'That's better,' the BFG said. 'Now I is hearing you very nicely. What is it you is trying to say to me just now?'

'I was saying are we ready?'

'We is off!' cried the BFG, heading for the cave entrance. 'We is off to meet Her Majester the Queen!'

Outside the cave, he rolled the large round stone back into place and set off at a tremendous gallop.

Journey to London

The great yellow wasteland lay dim and milky in the moonlight as the Big Friendly Giant went galloping across it.

Sophie, still wearing only her nightie, was reclining comfortably in a crevice of the BFG's right ear. She was actually in the outer rim of the ear, near the top, where the edge of the ear folds over, and this folding-over bit made a sort of roof for her and gave her wonderful protection against the rushing wind. What is more, she was lying on skin that was soft and warm and almost velvety. Nobody, she told herself, had ever travelled in greater comfort.

Sophie peeped over the rim of the ear and watched the desolate landscape of Giant Country go whizzing by. They were certainly moving fast. The BFG went bouncing off the ground as though there were rockets in his toes and each stride he took lifted him about a hundred feet into the air. But he had not yet gone into that whizzing top gear of his, when the ground became blurred by speed and the wind howled and his feet didn't seem to be touching anything but air. That would come later.

Sophie had not slept for a long time. She was very tired. She was also warm and comfortable. She dozed off.

She didn't know how long she slept, but when she woke up again and looked out over the edge of the ear, the landscape had changed completely. They were in a green country now, with mountains and forests. It was still dark but the moon was shining as brightly as ever.

Suddenly and without slowing his pace, the BFG turned his head sharply to the left. For the first time during the entire journey he spoke a few words. 'Look quick-quick over there,' he said, pointing his long trumpet.

Sophie looked in the direction he was pointing. Through the murky darkness all she saw at first was a great cloud of dust about three hundred yards away.

'Those is the other giants all galloping back home after their guzzle,' the BFG said.

Then Sophie saw them. In the light of the moon, she saw all nine of those monstrous half-naked brutes thundering across the landscape together. They were galloping in a pack, their necks craned forward, their arms bent at the elbows, and worst of all, their stomachs bulging. The strides they took were incredible. Their speed was unbelievable. Their feet pounded and thundered on the ground and left a great sheet of dust behind them. But in ten seconds they were gone.

'A lot of little girlsies and boysies is no longer sleeping in their beds tonight,' the BFG said.

Sophie felt quite ill.

But this grim encounter made her more than ever determined to go through with her mission.

It must have been about an hour or so later that the BFG began to slow his pace. 'We is in England now,' he said suddenly.

Dark though it was, Sophie could see that they were in a country of green fields with neat hedges in between the fields. There were hills with trees all over them and occasionally there were roads with the lights of cars moving along. Each time they came to a road, the BFG was over it and away, and no motorist could possibly have seen anything except a quick black shadow flashing overhead.

All at once, a curious orange-coloured glow appeared in the night sky ahead of them.

'We is coming close to London,' the BFG said.

He slowed to a trot. He began looking about cautiously.

Groups of houses were now appearing on all sides. But there were still no lights in their windows. It was too early for anyone to be getting up yet.

'Someone's bound to see us,' Sophie said.

'Never is they seeing me,' the BFG said confidently. 'You is forgetting that I is doing this sort of thing for years and years and years. No human bean is ever catching even the smallest wink of me.'

'I did,' Sophie whispered.

'Ah,' he said. 'Yes. But you was the very first.'

During the next half-hour, things moved so swiftly and so silently that Sophie, crouching in the giant's ear, was unable to understand exactly what was going on. They were in streets. There were houses everywhere. Sometimes there were shops. There were bright lamps in the streets. There were quite a few people about and there were cars with lights on. But nobody ever noticed the BFG. It was impossible to understand quite how he did it. There was a kind of magic in his movements. He seemed to melt into the shadows. He would glide – that was the only word to describe his way of moving – he would glide noiselessly from one dark place to another, always moving, always gliding forward through the streets of London. his black cloak blending with the shadows of the night.

It is quite possible that one or two late-night wanderers might have thought they saw a tall black shadow skimming swiftly down a murky sidestreet, but even if they had, they would never have believed their own eyes. They would have dismissed it as an illusion and blamed themselves for seeing things that weren't there.

Sophie and the BFG came at last to a large place full of trees. There was a road running through it, and a lake. There were no people in this place and the BFG stopped for the first time since they had set out from his cave many hours before.

'What's the matter?' Sophie whispered in her under-the-breath voice.

'I is in a bit of a puddle,' he said.

'You're doing marvellously,' Sophie whispered.

'No, I isn't,' he said. 'I is now completely boggled. I is lost.'

'But why?'

'Because we is meant to be in the middle of London and suddenly we is in green pastures.'

'Don't be silly,' Sophie whispered. 'This *is* the middle of London. It's called Hyde Park. I know exactly where we are.'

'You is joking.'

'I'm not. I swear I'm not. We're almost there.'

'You mean we is nearly at the Queen's Palace?' cried the BFG.

'It's just across the road,' Sophie whispered. 'This is where *I* take over.'

'Which way?' the BFG asked.

'Straight ahead.'

The BFG trotted forward through the deserted park.

'Now stop.'

The BFG stopped.

'You see that huge roundabout ahead of us just outside the Park?' Sophie whispered.

'I see it.'

'That is Hyde Park Corner.'

Even now, when it was still an hour before dawn, there was quite a lot of traffic moving around Hyde Park Corner.

Then Sophie whispered, 'In the middle of the roundabout there is an enormous stone arch with a statue of a horse and rider on top of it. Can you see that?'

The BFG peered through the trees. 'I is seeing it,' he said.

'Do you think that if you took a very fast run at it, you could jump clear over Hyde Park Corner, over the arch and over the horse and rider and land on the pavement the other side?'

'Easy,' the BFG said.

'You're sure? You're absolutely sure?'

'I promise,' the BFG said.

'Whatever you do, you mustn't land in the middle of Hyde Park Corner.'

'Don't get so flussed,' the BFG said. 'To me that is a snitchy little jump. There's not a thingalingaling to it.'

'Then *go!*' Sophie whispered.

The BFG broke into a full gallop. He went scorching

across the Park and just before he reached the railings that divided it from the street, he took off. It was a gigantic leap. He flew high over Hyde Park Corner and landed as softly as a cat on the pavement the other side.

'Well *done!*' Sophie whispered. 'Now quick! Over that wall!'

Directly in front of them, bordering the pavement, there was a brick wall with fearsome-looking spikes all along the top of it. A swift crouch, a little leap and the B F G was over it.

'We're there!' Sophie whispered excitedly. 'We're in the Queen's back garden!'

The Palace

'By gumdrops!' whispered the Big Friendly Giant. 'Is this really it?'

'There's the Palace,' Sophie whispered back.

Not more than a hundred yards away, through the tall trees in the garden, across the mown lawns and the tidy flower-beds, the massive shape of the Palace itself loomed through the darkness. It was made of whitish stone. The sheer size of it staggered the BFG.

'But this place is having a hundred bedrooms at least!' he said.

'Easily, I should think,' Sophie whispered.

'Then I is boggled,' the BFG said. 'How is I possibly finding the one where the Queen is sleeping?'

'Let's go a bit closer and have a look,' Sophie whispered.

The BFG glided forward among the trees. Suddenly he stopped dead. The great ear in which Sophie was sitting began to swivel round. 'Hey!' Sophie whispered. 'You're going to tip me out!'

'Ssshh!' the BFG whispered back. 'I is hearing something!' He stopped behind a clump of bushes. He waited. The ear was still swinging this way and that. Sophie had to hang on tight to the side of it to save herself from tumbling out. The BFG pointed through a gap in the bushes, and there, not more than fifty yards away, she saw a man padding softly across the lawn. He had a guard-dog with him on a leash.

The BFG stayed as still as a stone. So did Sophie. The man and the dog walked on and disappeared into the darkness.

'You was telling me they has no soldiers in the back garden,' the BFG whispered.

'He wasn't a soldier,' Sophie whispered. 'He was some sort of a watchman. We'll have to be careful.'

'I is not too worried,' the BFG said. 'These wacksey big ears of mine is picking up even the noise of a man *breathing* the other side of this garden.'

'How much longer before it begins to get light?' Sophie whispered.

'Very short,' the BFG said. 'We must go pell-mell for leather now!'

He glided forward through the vast garden, and once again Sophie noticed how he seemed to melt into the shadows wherever he went. His feet made no sound at all, even when he was walking on gravel.

Suddenly, they were right up close against the back wall of the great Palace. The BFG's head was level with the upper windows one flight up, and Sophie, sitting in his ear, had the same view. In all the windows on that floor the curtains seemed to be drawn. There were no lights showing anywhere. In the distance they could hear the muted sound of traffic going round Hyde Park Corner.

The BFG stopped and put his other ear, the one Sophie wasn't sitting in, close to the first window.

'No,' he whispered.

'What are you listening for?' Sophie whispered back.

'For breathing,' the BFG whispered. 'I is able to tell if it is a man human bean or a lady by the breathing-voice. We has a man in there. Snortling a little bit, too.'

He glided on, flattening his tall, thin, black-cloaked body against the side of the building. He came to the next window. He listened.

'No,' he whispered.

He moved on.

'This room is empty,' he whispered.

He listened in at several more windows, but at each one he shook his head and moved on.

When he came to the window in the very centre of the Palace, he listened but did not move on. 'Ho-ho,' he whispered. 'We has a lady sleeping in there.'

Sophie felt a little quiver go running down her spine. 'But who?' she whispered back.

The BFG put a finger to his lips for silence. He reached up through the open window and parted the curtains ever so slightly.

The orange glow from the night-sky over London crept into the room and cast a glimmer of light on to its walls. It was a large room. A lovely room. A rich carpet. Gilded chairs. A dressing-table. A bed. And on the pillow of the bed lay the head of a sleeping woman.

Sophie suddenly found herself looking at a face she had seen on stamps and coins and in the newspapers all her life.

For a few seconds she was speechless.

'Is that her?' the BFG whispered.

'Yes,' Sophie whispered back.

The BFG wasted no time. First, and very carefully, he started to raise the lower half of the large window. The

BFG was an expert on windows. He had opened thousands of them over the years to blow his dreams into children's bedrooms. Some windows got stuck. Some were wobbly. Some creaked. He was pleased to find that the Queen's window slid upward like silk. He pushed up the lower half as far as it would go so as to leave a place on the sill for Sophie to sit.

Next, he closed the crack in the curtains.

Then, with finger and thumb, he lifted Sophie out of his ear and placed her on the window-ledge with her legs dangling just inside the room, but behind the curtains.

'Now don't you go tip-toppling backwards,' the BFG whispered. 'You must always be holding on tight with both hands to the inside of the window-sill.'

Sophie did as he said.

It was summertime in London and the night was not cold, but don't forget that Sophie was wearing only her thin nightie. She would have given anything for a dressing-gown, not just to keep her warm but to hide the whiteness of her nightie from watchful eyes in the garden below.

The BFG was taking the glass jar from the pocket of his cloak. He unscrewed the lid. Now, very cautiously, he poured the precious dream into the wide end of his trumpet. He steered the trumpet through the curtains, far into the room, aiming it at the place where he knew the bed to be. He took a deep breath. He puffed out his cheeks and *pooff*, he blew.

Now he was withdrawing the trumpet, sliding it out very very carefully, like a thermometer.

'Is you all right sitting there?' he whispered.

'Yes,' Sophie murmured. She was quite terrified, but

determined not to show it. She looked down over her shoulder. The ground seemed miles away. It was a nasty drop.

'How long will the dream take to work?' Sophie whispered.

'Some takes an hour,' the BFG whispered back. 'Some is quicker. Some is slower still. But it is sure to find her in the end.'

Sophie said nothing.

'I is going off to wait in the garden,' the BFG whispered. 'When you is wanting me, just call out my name and I is coming very quick.'

'Will you hear me?' Sophie whispered.

'You is forgetting these,' the BFG whispered, smiling and pointing to his great ears.

'Goodbye,' Sophie whispered.

Suddenly, unexpectedly, the BFG leaned forward and kissed her gently on the cheek.

Sophie felt like crying.

When she turned to look at him, he was already gone. He had simply melted away into the dark garden.

The Queen

Dawn came at last, and the rim of a lemon-coloured sun rose up behind the roof-tops somewhere behind Victoria Station.

A while later, Sophie felt a little of its warmth on her back and was grateful.

In the distance, she heard a church clock striking. She counted the strikes. There were seven.

She found it almost impossible to believe that she, Sophie, a little orphan of no real importance in the world, was at this moment actually sitting high above the ground on the window-sill of the Queen of England's bedroom, with the Queen herself asleep in there behind the curtain not more than five yards away.

The very idea of it was absurd.

No one had ever done such a thing before.

It was a terrifying thing to be doing.

What would happen if the dream didn't work?

No one, least of all the Queen, would believe a word of her story.

It seemed possible that nobody had ever woken up to find a small child sitting behind the curtains on his or her window-sill.

The Queen was bound to get a shock.

Who wouldn't?

With all the patience of a small girl who has something

important to wait for, Sophie sat motionless on the window-sill.

How much longer? she wondered.

What time do Queens wake up?

Faint stirrings and distant sounds came to her from deep inside the belly of the Palace.

Then, all at once, beyond the curtains, she heard the voice of the sleeper in the bedroom. It was a slightly blurred sleep-talker's voice. 'Oh no!' it cried out. 'No! Don't – Someone stop them! – Don't let them do it! – I can't bear it! – Oh please stop them! – It's horrible! – Oh, it's ghastly! – No! No! No! . . .'

She is having the dream, Sophie told herself. It must be really horrid. I feel so sorry for her. But it has to be done.

After that, there were a few moans. Then there was a long silence.

Sophie waited. She looked over her shoulder. She was terrified that she would see the man with the dog down in the garden staring up at her. But the garden was deserted. A pale summer mist hung over it like smoke. It was an enormous garden, very beautiful, with a large funny-shaped lake at the far end. There was an island in the lake and there were ducks swimming on the water.

Inside the room, beyond the curtains, Sophie suddenly heard what was obviously a knock on the door. She heard the doorknob being turned. She heard someone entering the room.

'Good morning, Your Majesty,' a woman was saying. It was the voice of an oldish person.

There was a pause and then a slight rattle of china and silver.

148

'Will you have your tray on the bed, ma'am, or on the table?'

'Oh Mary! Something awful has just happened!' This was a voice Sophie had heard many times on radio and television, especially on Christmas Day. It was a very well-known voice.

'Whatever is it, ma'am?'

'I've just had the most frightful dream! It was a nightmare! It was awful!'

'Oh, I am sorry, ma'am. But don't be distressed. You're awake now and it will go away. It *was* only a dream, ma'am.'

'Do you know what I dreamt, Mary? I dreamt that girls and boys were being snatched out of their beds at boarding-school and were being eaten by the most ghastly giants! The giants were putting their arms in through the dormitory windows and plucking the children out with their fingers! One lot from a girls' school and another from a boys' school! It was all so . . . so *vivid*, Mary! It was so *real*!'

There was a silence. Sophie waited. She was quivering with excitement. But why the silence? Why didn't the other one, the maid, why didn't she say something?

'What on earth's the matter, Mary?' the famous voice was saying.

There was another silence.

'Mary! You've gone as white as a sheet! Are you feeling ill?'

There was suddenly a crash and a clatter of crockery which could only have meant that the tray the maid was carrying had fallen out of her hands.

'Mary!' the famous voice was saying rather sharply. 'I

think you'd better sit down at once! You look as though you're going to faint! You really mustn't take it so hard just because I've had an awful dream.'

'That ... that ... that isn't the reason, ma'am.' The maid's voice was quivering terribly.

'Then for heaven's sake what *is* the reason?'

'I'm very sorry about the tray, ma'am.'

'Oh, don't worry about the *tray*. But what on earth was it that made you drop it? Why did you go white as a ghost all of a sudden?'

'You haven't seen the papers yet, have you, ma'am?'

'No, what do they say?'

Sophie heard the rustling of a newspaper as it was being handed over.

'It's like the very dream you had in the night, ma'am.'

'Rubbish, Mary. Where is it?'

'On the front page, ma'am. It's the big headlines.'

'Great Scott!' cried the famous voice. 'Eighteen girls vanish mysteriously from their beds at Roedean School! Fourteen boys disappear from Eton! Bones are found underneath dormitory windows!'

Then there was a pause punctuated by gasps from the famous voice as the newspaper article was clearly being read and digested.

'Oh, how ghastly!' the famous voice cried out. 'It's *absolutely* frightful! Bones under the windows! What *can* have happened? Oh, those *poor* children!'

'But ma'am ... don't you see, ma'am ...'

'See what, Mary?'

'Those children were taken away almost exactly as you dreamt it, ma'am!'

'Not by giants, Mary.'

'No, ma'am. But the bit about the girls and boys disappearing from their dormitories, you dreamt it so clearly and then it actually happened. That's why I came over all queer, ma'am.'

'I'm coming over a bit queer myself, Mary.'

'It gives me the shakes, ma'am, when something like that happens, it really does.'

'I don't blame you, Mary.'

'I shall get you some more breakfast, ma'am, and have this mess cleared up.'

'No! Don't go, Mary! Stay here a moment!'

Sophie wished she could see into the room, but she didn't dare touch the curtains. The famous voice began speaking again. 'I really *did* dream about those children, Mary. It was clear as crystal.'

'I know you did, ma'am.'

'I don't know how *giants* got into it. That was rubbish.'

'Shall I draw the curtains, ma'am, then we shall all feel better. It's a lovely day.'

'Please do.'

With a swish, the great curtains were pulled aside.

The maid screamed.

Sophie froze to the window-ledge.

The Queen, sitting up in her bed with *The Times* on her lap, glanced up sharply. Now it was *her* turn to freeze. She didn't scream as the maid had done. Queens are too self-controlled for that. She simply sat there staring wide-eyed and white-faced at the small girl who was perched on her window-sill in a nightie.

Sophie was petrified.

Curiously enough, the Queen looked petrified, too. One would have expected her to look surprised, as you

or I would have done had we discovered a small girl
sitting on our window-sill first thing in the morning. But
the Queen didn't look surprised. She looked genuinely
frightened.

The maid, a middle-aged woman with a funny cap on
the top of her head, was the first to recover. 'What in the
name of heaven do you think you're doing in here?' she
shouted angrily to Sophie.

Sophie looked beseechingly towards the Queen for help.

The Queen was still staring at Sophie. Gaping at her would be more accurate. Her mouth was slightly open, her eyes were round and wide as two saucers, and the whole of that famous rather lovely face was filled with disbelief.

'Now listen here, young lady, how on earth did you get into this room?' the maid shouted furiously.

'I don't believe it,' the Queen was murmuring. 'I simply don't believe it.'

'I'll take her out, ma'am, at once,' the maid was saying.

'No, Mary! No, don't do that!' The Queen spoke so sharply that the maid was quite taken aback. She turned

and stared at the Queen. What on earth had come over her? It looked as though she was in a state of shock.

'Are you all right, ma'am?' the maid was saying.

When the Queen spoke again, it was in a strange strangled sort of whisper. 'Tell me, Mary,' she said, 'tell me quite truthfully, is there *really* a little girl sitting on my window-sill, or am I still dreaming?'

'She is sitting there all right, ma'am, as clear as daylight, but heaven only knows how she got there! Your Majesty is certainly not dreaming it this time!'

'But that's exactly what I *did* dream!' the Queen cried out. 'I dreamt that *as well*! I dreamt there would be a little girl sitting on my window-sill in her nightie and she would talk to me!'

The maid, with her hands clasped across her starched white bosom, was staring at her mistress with a look of absolute disbelief on her face. The situation was getting beyond her. She was lost. She had not been trained to cope with this kind of madness.

'Are you real?' the Queen said to Sophie.

'Y-y-yes, Your Majesty,' Sophie murmured.

'What is your name?'

'Sophie, Your Majesty.'

'And how did you get up on to my window-sill? No, don't answer that! Hang on a moment! I dreamed that part of it, too! I dreamed that a giant put you there!'

'He did, Your Majesty,' Sophie said.

The maid gave a howl of anguish and clasped her hands over her face.

'Control yourself, Mary,' the Queen said sharply. Then to Sophie she said, 'You are not serious about the giant, are you?'

'Oh yes, Your Majesty. He's out there in the garden now.'

'Is he indeed,' the Queen said. The sheer absurdity of it all was helping her to regain her composure. 'So he's in the garden, is he?' she said, smiling a little.

'He is a *good* giant, Your Majesty,' Sophie said. 'You need not be frightened of him.'

'I'm delighted to hear it,' said the Queen, still smiling.

'He is my best friend, Your Majesty.'

'How nice,' the Queen said.

'He's a lovely giant, Your Majesty.'

'I'm quite sure he is,' the Queen said. 'But why have you and this giant come to see me?'

'I think you have dreamed that part of it, too, Your Majesty,' Sophie said calmly.

That pulled the Queen up short.

It took the smile right off her face.

She certainly *had* dreamed that part of it. She was remembering now how, at the end of her dream, it had said that a little girl and a big friendly giant would come and show her how to find the nine horrible man-eating giants.

But be careful, the Queen told herself. Keep very calm. Because this is surely not very far from the place where madness begins.

'You *did* dream that, didn't you, Your Majesty?' Sophie said.

The maid was out of it now. She just stood there goggling.

'Yes,' the Queen murmured. 'Yes, now you come to mention it, I did. But how do *you* know what I dreamed?'

'Oh, that's a long story, Your Majesty,' Sophie said. 'Would you like me to call the Big Friendly Giant?'

The Queen looked at the child. The child looked straight back at the Queen, her face open and quite serious. The Queen simply didn't know what to make of it. Was someone pulling her leg, she wondered.

'Shall I call him for you?' Sophie went on. 'You'll like him very much.'

The Queen took a deep breath. She was glad no one except her faithful old Mary was here to see what was going on. 'Very well,' she said. 'You may call your giant. No, wait a moment. Mary, pull yourself together and give me my dressing-gown and slippers.'

The maid did as she was told. The Queen got out of bed and put on a pale pink dressing-gown and slippers.

'You may call him now,' the Queen said.

Sophie turned her head towards the garden and called out, 'BFG! Her Majesty The Queen would like to see you!'

The Queen crossed over to the window and stood beside Sophie.

'Come down off that ledge,' she said. 'You're going to fall backwards any moment.'

Sophie jumped down into the room and stood beside the Queen at the open window. Mary, the maid, stood behind them. Her hands were now planted firmly on her hips and there was a look on her face which seemed to say, 'I want no part of this fiasco.'

'I don't see any giant,' the Queen said.

'Please wait,' Sophie said.

'Shall I take her away now, ma'am?' the maid said.

'Take her downstairs and give her some breakfast,' the Queen said.

Just then, there was a rustle in the bushes beside the lake.

Then out he came!

Twenty-four feet tall, wearing his black cloak with the grace of a nobleman, still carrying his long trumpet in one hand, he strode magnificently across the Palace lawn towards the window.

The maid screamed.

The Queen gasped.

Sophie waved.

The BFG took his time. He was very dignified in his approach. When he was close to the window where the three of them were standing, he stopped and made a slow graceful bow. His head, after he had straightened up again, was almost exactly level with the watchers at the window.

'Your Majester,' he said. 'I is your humbug servant.' He bowed again.

Considering she was meeting a giant for the first time in her life, the Queen remained astonishingly self-composed. 'We are very pleased to meet you,' she said.

Down below, a gardener was coming across the lawn

with a wheelbarrow. He caught sight of the BFG's legs over to his left. His gaze travelled slowly upwards along the entire height of the enormous body. He gripped the handles of the wheelbarrow. He swayed. He tottered. Then he keeled over on the grass in a dead faint. Nobody noticed him.

'Oh, Majester!' cried the BFG. 'Oh, Queen! Oh Monacher! Oh, Golden Sovereign! Oh, Ruler! Oh, Ruler of Straight Lines! Oh, Sultana! I is come here with my little friend Sophie ... to give you a ...' The BFG hesitated, searching for the word.

'To give me *what?*' the Queen said.

'A *sistance*,' the BFG said, beaming.

The Queen looked puzzled.

'He sometimes speaks a bit funny, Your Majesty,' Sophie said. 'He never went to school.'

'Then we must send him to school,' the Queen said. 'We have some very good schools in this country.'

'I has great secrets to tell Your Majester,' the BFG said.

'I should be delighted to hear them,' the Queen said. 'But not in my dressing-gown.'

'Shall you wish to get dressed, ma'am?' the maid said.

'Have either of you had breakfast?' the Queen said.

'Oh, *could we?*' Sophie cried. 'Oh, *please!* I haven't eaten a thing since yesterday!'

'I was about to have mine,' the Queen said, 'but Mary dropped it.'

The maid gulped.

'I imagine we have more food in the Palace,' the Queen said, speaking to the BFG. 'Perhaps you and your little friend would care to join me.'

'Will it be repulsant snozzcumbers, Majester?' the BFG asked.

'Will it be *what?*' the Queen said.

'Stinky snozzcumbers,' the BFG said.

'What *is* he talking about?' the Queen said. 'It sounds like a rude word to me.' She turned to the maid and said, 'Mary, ask them to serve breakfast for three in the . . . I think it had better be in the Ballroom. That has the highest ceiling.' To the BFG, she said, 'I'm afraid you will have to go through the door on your hands and knees. I shall send someone to show you the way.'

The BFG reached up and lifted Sophie out of the window. 'You and I is leaving Her Majester alone to get dressed,' he said.

'No, leave the little girl here with me,' the Queen said. 'We'll have to find something for her to put on. She can't have breakfast in her nightie.'

The BFG returned Sophie to the bedroom.

'Can we have sausages, Your Majesty?' Sophie said. 'And bacon and fried eggs?'

'I think that might be managed,' the Queen answered, smiling.

'Just you wait till you taste it!' Sophie said to the BFG. 'No more snozzcumbers from now on!'

The Royal Breakfast

There was a frantic scurry among the Palace servants when orders were received from the Queen that a twenty-four-foot giant must be seated with Her Majesty in the Great Ballroom within the next half-hour.

The butler, an imposing personage named Mr Tibbs, was in supreme command of all the palace servants and he did the best he could in the short time available. A man does not rise to become the Queen's butler unless he is gifted with extraordinary ingenuity, adaptability, versatility, dexterity, cunning, sophistication, sagacity, discretion and a host of other talents that neither you nor I possess. Mr Tibbs had them all. He was in the butler's pantry sipping an early morning glass of light ale when the order reached him. In a split second he had made the following calculations in his head: if a normal six-foot man requires a three-foot-high table to eat off, a twenty-four-foot giant will require a twelve-foot-high table.

And if a six foot man requires a chair with a two-foot-high seat, a twenty-four-foot giant will require a chair with an eight-foot-high seat.

Everything, Mr Tibbs told himself, must be multiplied by four. Two breakfast eggs must become eight. Four rashers of bacon must become sixteen. Three pieces of toast must become twelve, and so on. These calculations about food were immediately passed on to Monsieur Papillion, the royal chef.

Mr Tibbs skimmed into the ballroom (butlers don't walk, they skim over the ground) followed by a whole army of footmen. The footmen all wore knee-breeches and every one of them displayed beautifully rounded calves and ankles. There is no way you can become a royal footman unless you have a well-turned ankle. It is the first thing they look at when you are interviewed.

'Push the grand piano into the centre of the room,' Mr Tibbs whispered. Butlers never raise their voices above the softest whisper.

Four footmen moved the piano.

'Now fetch a large chest-of-drawers and put it on top of the piano,' Mr Tibbs whispered.

Three other footmen fetched a very fine Chippendale mahogany chest-of-drawers and placed it on top of the piano.

'That will be his chair,' Mr Tibbs whispered. 'It is exactly eight feet off the ground. Now we shall make a table upon which this gentleman may eat his breakfast in comfort. Fetch me four very tall grandfather clocks. There are plenty of them around the Palace. Let each clock be twelve feet high.'

Sixteen footmen spread out around the Palace to find the clocks. They were not easy to carry and required four footmen to each one.

'Place the four clocks in a rectangle eight feet by four alongside the grand piano,' Mr Tibbs whispered.

The footmen did so.

'Now fetch me the young Prince's ping-pong table,' Mr Tibbs whispered.

The ping-pong table was carried in.

'Unscrew its legs and take them away,' Mr Tibbs whispered. This was done.

'Now place the ping-pong table on top of the four grandfather clocks,' Mr Tibbs whispered. To manage this, the footmen had to stand on stepladders.

Mr Tibbs stood back to survey the new furniture. 'None of it is in the classic style,' he whispered, 'but it will have to do.' He gave orders that a damask table-cloth should be draped over the ping-pong table, and in the end it looked really quite elegant after all.

At this point, Mr Tibbs was seen to hesitate. The footmen all stared at him, aghast. Butlers never hesitate, not even when they are faced with the most impossible problems. It is their job to be totally decisive at all times.

'Knives and forks and spoons,' Mr Tibbs was heard to mutter. 'Our cutlery will be like little pins in his hands.'

But Mr Tibbs didn't hesitate for long. 'Tell the head gardener,' he whispered, 'that I require immediately a brand new unused garden fork and also a spade. And for a knife we shall use the great sword hanging on the wall in the morning-room. But clean the sword well first. It was last used to cut off the head of King Charles the First and there may still be a little dried blood on the blade.'

When all this had been accomplished, Mr Tibbs stood near the centre of the Ballroom casting his expert butler's eye over the scene. Had he forgotten anything? He certainly had. What about a coffee cup for the large gentleman?

'Fetch me,' he whispered, 'the biggest jug you can find in the kitchen.'

A splendid one gallon porcelain water-jug was brought in and placed on the giant's table beside the garden fork and the garden spade and the great sword.

So much for the giant.

Mr Tibbs then had the footmen move a small delicate table and two chairs alongside the giant's table. This was for the Queen and for Sophie. The fact that the giant's table and chair towered far above the smaller table simply could not be helped.

All these arrangements were only just completed when the Queen, now fully dressed in a trim skirt and cashmere cardigan, entered the Ballroom holding Sophie by the hand. A pretty blue dress that had once belonged to one of the Princesses had been found for Sophie, and to make her look prettier still, the Queen had picked up a superb sapphire brooch from her dressing-table and had pinned it on the left side of Sophie's chest. The Big Friendly Giant followed behind them, but he had an awful job getting through the door. He had to squeeze himself through on his hands and knees, with two footmen pushing him from behind and two pulling from the front. But he got through in the end. He had removed his black cloak and got rid of his trumpet, and was now wearing his ordinary simple clothes.

As he walked across the Ballroom he had to stoop quite a lot to avoid hitting the ceiling. Because of this he failed to notice an enormous crystal chandelier. *Crash* went his head right into the chandelier. A shower of glass fell upon the poor BFG. 'Gunghummers and bogswinkles!' he cried. 'What was that?'

'It *was* Louis the Fifteenth,' the Queen said, looking slightly put out.

'He's never been in a house before,' Sophie said.

Mr Tibbs scowled. He directed four footmen to clear up the mess, then, with a disdainful little wave of the hand, he indicated to the giant that he should seat himself on top of the chest-of-drawers on top of the grand piano.

'What a phizz-whizzing flushbunking seat!' cried the BFG. 'I is going to be bug as a snug in a rug up here.'

'Does he always speak like that?' the Queen asked.

'Quite often,' Sophie said. 'He gets tangled up with his words.'

The BFG sat down on the chest-of-drawers-piano and gazed in wonder around the Great Ballroom. 'By gumdrops!' he cried. 'What a spliffling whoppsy room we is in! It is so gigantuous I is needing bicirculers and telescoops to see what is going on at the other end!'

Footmen arrived carrying silver trays with fried eggs, bacon, sausages and fried potatoes.

At this point, Mr Tibbs suddenly realized that in order

to serve the BFG at his twelve-foot-high-grandfather-clock table, he would have to climb to the top of one of the tall step-ladders. What's more, he must do it balancing a huge warm plate on the palm of one hand and holding a gigantic silver coffee-pot in the other. A normal man would have flinched at the thought of it. But good butlers never flinch. Up he went, up and up and up, while the Queen and Sophie watched him with great interest. It is possible they were both secretly hoping he would lose his balance and go crashing to the floor. But good butlers never crash.

At the top of the ladder, Mr Tibbs, balancing like an acrobat, poured the BFG's coffee and placed the enormous plate before him. On the plate there were eight eggs, twelve sausages, sixteen rashers of bacon and a heap of fried potatoes.

'What is this please, Your Majester?' the BFG asked, peering down at the Queen.

'He has never eaten anything except snozzcumbers

before in his life,' Sophie explained. 'They taste revolting.'

'They don't seem to have stunted his growth,' the Queen said.

The BFG grabbed the garden spade and scooped up all the eggs, sausages, bacon and potatoes in one go and shovelled them into his enormous mouth.

'By goggles!' he cried. 'This stuff is making snozzcumbers taste like swatchwallop!'

The Queen glanced up, frowning. Mr Tibbs looked down at his toes and his lips moved in silent prayer.

'That was only one titchy little bite,' the BFG said. 'Is you having any more of this delunctious grubble in your cupboard, Majester?'

'Tibbs,' the Queen said, showing true regal hospitality, 'fetch the gentleman another dozen fried eggs and a dozen sausages.'

Mr Tibbs swam out of the room muttering unspeakable words to himself and wiping his brow with a white handkerchief.

The BFG lifted the huge jug and took a swallow. 'Owch!' he cried, blowing a mouthful across the ballroom. 'Please, what is this horrible swigpill I is drinking, Majester?'

'It's coffee,' the Queen told him. 'Freshly roasted.'

'It's filthsome!' the BFG cried out. 'Where is the frobscottle?'

'The *what?*' the Queen asked.

'Delumptious fizzy frobscottle,' the BFG answered. 'Everyone must be drinking frobscottle with breakfast, Majester. Then we can all be whizzpopping happily together afterwards.'

'What *does* he mean?' the Queen said, frowning at Sophie. 'What is whizzpopping?'

Sophie kept a very straight face. 'BFG,' she said, 'there is no frobscottle here and whizzpopping is strictly forbidden!'

'What!' cried the BFG. 'No frobscottle? No whizzpopping? No glumptious music? No boom-boom-boom?'

'Absolutely not,' Sophie told him firmly.

'If he wants to sing, please don't stop him,' the Queen said.

'He doesn't want to sing,' Sophie said.

'He said he wants to make music,' the Queen went on. 'Shall I send for a violin?'

'No, Your Majesty,' Sophie said. 'He's only joking.'

A sly little smile crossed the BFG's face. 'Listen,' he said, peering down at Sophie, 'if they isn't having any frobscottle here in the Palace, I can still go whizzpopping perfectly well without it if I is trying hard enough.'

'No!' cried Sophie. 'Don't! You're not to! I beg you!'

'Music is very good for the digestion,' the Queen said. 'When I'm up in Scotland, they play the bagpipes outside the window while I'm eating. Do play something.'

'I has Her Majester's permission!' cried the BFG, and all at once he let fly with a whizzpopper that sounded as though a bomb had exploded in the room.

The Queen jumped.

'Whoopee!' shouted the BFG. 'That is better than bagglepipes, is it not, Majester?'

It took the Queen a few seconds to get over the shock. 'I prefer the bagpipes,' she said. But she couldn't stop herself smiling.

During the next twenty minutes, a whole relay of

footmen were kept busy hurrying to and from the kitchen carrying third helpings and fourth helpings and fifth helpings of fried eggs and sausages for the ravenous and delighted BFG.

When the BFG had consumed his seventy-second fried egg, Mr Tibbs sidled up to the Queen. He bent low from the waist and whispered in her ear, 'Chef sends his apologies, Your Majesty, and he says he has no more eggs in the kitchen.'

'What's wrong with the hens?' the Queen said.

'Nothing's wrong with the hens, Your Majesty,' Mr Tibbs whispered.

'Then tell them to lay more,' the Queen said. She looked up at the BFG. 'Have some toast and marmalade while you're waiting,' she said to him.

'The toast is finished,' Mr Tibbs whispered, 'and chef says there is no more bread.'

'Tell him to bake more,' the Queen said.

While all this was going on, Sophie had been telling the Queen everything, absolutely everything about her visit to Giant Country. The Queen listened, appalled. When Sophie had finished, the Queen looked up at the BFG who was sitting high above her. He was now eating a sponge-cake.

'Big Friendly Giant,' she said, 'last night those man-eating brutes came to England. Can you remember where they went the night before?'

The BFG put a whole round sponge-cake into his mouth and chewed it slowly while he thought about this question. 'Yes, Majester,' he said. 'I do think I is remembering where they said they was going the night before last. They was galloping off to Sweden for the Sweden sour taste.'

'Fetch me a telephone,' the Queen commanded.

Mr Tibbs placed the instrument on the table. The Queen lifted the receiver. 'Get me the King of Sweden,' she said.

'Good morning,' the Queen said. 'Is everything all right in Sweden?'

'Everything is terrible!' the King of Sweden answered. 'There is panic in the capital! Two nights ago, twenty-six of my loyal subjects disappeared! My whole country is in in a panic!'

'Your twenty-six loyal subjects were all eaten by giants,' the Queen said. 'Apparently they like the taste of Swedes.'

'Why do they like the taste of Swedes?' the King asked.

'Because the Swedes of Sweden have a sweet and sour taste. So says the BFG,' the Queen said.

'I don't know *what* you're talking about,' the King said, growing testy. 'It's hardly a joking matter when one's loyal subjects are being eaten like popcorn.'

'They've eaten mine as well,' the Queen said.

'Who's *they*, for heaven's sake?' the King asked.

'Giants,' the Queen said.

'Look here,' the King said, 'are you feeling all right?'

'It's been a rough morning,' the Queen said. 'First I had a horrid nightmare, then the maid dropped my breakfast and now I've got a giant on the piano.'

'You need a doctor quick!' cried the King.

'I'll be all right,' the Queen said. 'I must go now. Thanks for your help.' She replaced the receiver.

'Your BFG is right,' the Queen said to Sophie. 'Those nine man-eating brutes *did* go to Sweden.'

'It's horrible,' Sophie said. 'Please stop them, Your Majesty.'

'I'd like to make one more check before I call out the troops,' the Queen said. Once more, she looked up at the BFG. He was eating doughnuts now, popping them into his mouth ten at a time, like peas. 'Think hard, BFG,' she said. 'Where did those horrid giants say they were galloping off to *three* nights ago?'

The BFG thought long and hard.

'Ho-ho!' he cried at last. 'Yes, I is remembering!'

'Where?' asked the Queen.

'One was off to Baghdad,' the BFG said. 'As they is galloping past my cave, Fleshlumpeater is waving his arms and shouting at me, "I is off to Baghdad and I is going to Baghdad and mum and every one of their ten children as well!"'

Once more, the Queen lifted the receiver. 'Get me the Lord Mayor of Baghdad,' she said. 'If they don't have a Lord Mayor, get me the next best thing.'

In five seconds, a voice was on the line. 'Here is the Sultan of Baghdad speaking,' the voice said.

'Listen, Sultan,' the Queen said. 'Did anything unpleasant happen in your city three nights ago?'

'Every night unpleasant things are happening in Baghdad,' the Sultan said. 'We are chopping off people's heads like you are chopping parsley.'

'I've never chopped parsley in my life,' the Queen said. 'I want to know if anyone has *disappeared* recently in Baghdad?'

'Only my uncle, Caliph Haroun al Rashid,' the Sultan

said. 'He disappeared from his bed three nights ago together with his wife and ten children.'

'There you is!' cried the BFG, whose wonderful ears enabled him to hear what the Sultan was saying to the Queen on the telephone. 'Fleshlumpeater did that one! He went off to Baghdad to bag dad and mum and all the little kiddles!'

The Queen replaced the receiver. 'That proves it,' she said, looking up at the BFG. 'Your story is apparently quite true. Summon the Head of the Army and the Head of the Air Force immediately!'

The Plan

The Head of the Army and the Head of the Air Force stood at attention beside the Queen's breakfast table. Sophie was still in her seat and the BFG was still high up on his crazy perch.

It took the Queen only five minutes to explain the situation to the military men.

'I *knew* there was something like this going on, Your Majesty,' the Head of the Army said. 'For the last ten years we have been getting reports from nearly every country in the world about people disappearing mysteriously in the night. We had one only the other day from Panama . . .'

'For the hatty taste!' cried the BFG.

'And one from Wellington, in New Zealand,' said the Head of the Army.

'For the booty flavour!' cried the BFG.

'What *is* he talking about?' said the Head of the Air Force.

'Work it out for yourself,' the Queen said. 'What time is it? Ten a.m. In eight hours those nine blood-thirsty brutes will be galloping off to gobble up another couple of dozen unfortunate wretches. They have to be stopped. We must act fast.'

'We'll bomb the blighters!' shouted the Head of the Air Force.

'We'll mow them down with machine-guns!' cried the Head of the Army.

'I do not approve of murder,' the Queen said.

'But they are murderers themselves!' cried the Head of the Army.

'That is no reason why we should follow their example,' the Queen said. 'Two wrongs don't make a right.'

'And two rights don't make a left!' cried the BFG.

'We must bring them back alive,' the Queen said.

'How?' the two military men said together. 'They are all fifty feet high. They'd knock us down like ninepins!'

'Wait!' cried the BFG. 'Hold your horseflies! Keep your skirts on! I think I has the answer to the maiden's hair!'

'Let him speak,' the Queen said.

'Every afternoon,' the BFG said, 'all these giants is in the Land of Noddy.'

'I can't understand a word this feller says,' the Head of the Army snapped. 'Why doesn't he speak clearly?'

'He means the Land of Nod,' Sophie said. 'It's pretty obvious.'

'Exunckly!' cried the BFG. 'Every afternoon all these nine giants is lying on the ground snoozling away in a very deep sleep. They is always resting like that before they is galloping off to guzzle another helping of human beans.'

'Go on,' they said. 'So what?'

'So what you soldiers has to do is to creep up to the giants while they is still in the Land of Noddy and tie their arms and legs with mighty ropes and whunking chains.'

'Brilliant,' the Queen said.

'That's all very well,' said the Head of the Army. 'But how do we get the brutes back here? We can't load fifty-foot giants on to trucks! Shoot 'em on the spot, that's what I say!'

The BFG looked down from his lofty perch and said, this time to the Head of the Air Force, 'You is.having bellypoppers, is you not?'

'Is he being rude?' the Head of the Air Force said.

'He means helicopters,' Sophie told him.

'Then why doesn't he say so? Of course we have helicopters.'

'Whoppsy big bellypoppers?' asked the BFG.

'Very big ones,' the Head of the Air Force said proudly. 'But no helicopter is big enough to get a giant like that inside it.'

'You do not put him inside,' the BFG said. 'You sling him underneath the belly of your bellypopper and carry him like a porteedo.'

'Like a *what*?' said the Head of the Air Force.

'Like a torpedo,' Sophie said.

'Could you do that, Air Marshal?' the Queen asked.

'Well, I suppose we *could*,' the Head of the Air Force admitted grudgingly.

'Then get cracking!' the Queen said, 'You'll need nine helicopters, one for each Giant.'

'Where is this place?' the Air Force man said to the BFG. 'I presume you can pinpoint it on the map?'

'*Pinpoint?*' said the BFG. '*Map?* I is never hearing these words before. Is this Air Force bean talking slushbungle?'

The Air Marshal's face turned the colour of a ripe plum. He was not used to being told he was talking slushbungle. The Queen, with her usual admirable tact and good sense, came to the rescue. 'BFG,' she said, 'can you tell us *more or less* where this Giant Country is?'

'No, Majester,' the BFG said. 'Not on my nelly.'

'Then we're jiggered!' cried the Army General.

'This is ridiculous!' cried the Air Marshal.

'You must not be giving up so easy,' the BFG said calmly. 'The first titchy bobsticle you meet and you begin shouting you is biffsquiggled.'

The Army General was no more used to being insulted than the Air Marshal. His face began to swell with fury and his cheeks blew out until they looked like two huge ripe tomatoes. 'Your Majesty!' he cried. 'We are dealing with a lunatic! I want nothing more to do with this ridiculous operation!'

The Queen, who was used to the tantrums of her senior officials, ignored him completely. 'BFG,' she said, 'Would you please tell these rather dim-witted characters exactly what to do.'

'A pleasure, Majester,' said the BFG. 'Now listen to me carefully, you two bootbogglers.'

The military men began to twitch, but they stayed put.

'I is not having the foggiest idea where Giant Country is in the world,' the BFG said, 'but I is always able to gallop there. I is galloping forthwards and backwards from Giant Country every night to blow my dreams into little chiddler's bedrooms. I is knowing the way very well. So all you is having to do is this. Put your nine big bellyhoppers up in the air and let them follow me as I is galloping along.'

'How long will the journey take?' the Queen asked.

'If we is leaving now,' the BFG said, 'we will be arriving just as the giants is having their afternoon snozzle.'

'Splendid,' said the Queen. Then turning to the two

military men, she said, 'Prepare to leave immediately.'

The Head of the Army, who was feeling pretty miffed by the whole business, said, 'That's all very well, Your Majesty, but what are we going to do with the blighters once we've got them back?'

'Don't you worry about that,' the Queen told him. 'We'll be ready for them. Hurry up, now! Off you go!'

'If it pleases Your Majesty,' Sophie said, 'I should like to ride with the BFG, to keep him company.'

'Where will you sit?' asked the Queen.

'In his ear,' Sophie said. 'Show them, BFG.'

The BFG got down from his high chair. He picked Sophie up in his fingers. He swivelled his huge right ear until it was parallel with the ground, then he placed Sophie gently inside it.

The Heads of the Army and the Air Force stood there goggling. The Queen smiled. 'You really are rather a wonderful giant,' she said.

'Majester,' the BFG said, 'I is wishing to ask a very special thing from you.'

'What is it?' the Queen said.

'Could I please bring back here in the bellypoppers all my collection of dreams? They is taking me years and years to collect and I is not wanting to lose them.'

'Why of course,' the Queen said. 'I wish you a safe journey.'

The BFG had made thousands of journeys to and from Giant Country over the years, but he had never in his life made one quite like this, with nine huge helicopters roaring along just over his head. He had never before travelled in broad daylight either. He hadn't dared to.

But this was different. Now he was doing it for the Queen of England herself and he was frightened of nobody.

As he galloped across the British Isles with the helicopters thundering above him, people stood and gaped and wondered what on earth was going on. They had never seen the likes of it before. And they never would again.

Every now and then, the pilots of the helicopters would catch a glimpse of a small girl wearing glasses crouching in the giant's right ear and waving to them. They always waved back. The pilots marvelled at the giant's speed and at the way he leapt across wide rivers and over huge houses.

But they hadn't seen anything yet.

'Be careful to hang on tight!' the BFG said. 'We is going fast as a fizzlecrump!' The BFG changed into his famous top gear and all at once he began to fly forward as though there were springs in his legs and rockets in his toes. He went skimming over the earth like some magical hop-skip-and-jumper with his feet hardly ever touching the ground. As usual, Sophie had to crouch low in the crevice of his ear to save herself from being swept clean away.

The nine pilots in their helicopters suddenly realized they were being left behind. The giant was streaking ahead. They opened their throttles to full speed, and even then they were only just able to keep up.

In the leading machine, the Head of the Air Force was sitting beside the pilot. He had a world atlas on his knees and he kept staring first at the atlas, then at the ground below, trying to figure out where they were going. Frantically he turned the pages of the atlas. 'Where the devil *are* we going?' he cried.

'I haven't the foggiest idea,' the pilot answered. 'The Queen's orders were to follow the giant and that's exactly what I'm doing.'

The pilot was a young Air Force officer with a bushy

184

moustache. He was very proud of his moustache. He was also quite fearless and he loved adventure. He thought this was a super adventure. 'It's fun going to new places,' he said.

'*New places!*' shouted the Head of the Air Force. 'What the blazes d'you mean *new places?*'

'This place we're flying over now isn't in the atlas, is it?' the pilot said, grinning.

'You're darn right it isn't in the atlas!' cried the Head of the Air Force. 'We've flown clear off the last page!'

'I expect that old giant knows where he's going,' the young pilot said.

'He's leading us to disaster!' cried the Head of the Air Force. He was shaking with fear. In the seat behind him sat the Head of the Army who was even more terrified.

'You don't mean to tell me we've gone right out of the atlas?' he cried, leaning forward to look.

'That's exactly what I *am* telling you!' cried the Air Force man. 'Look for yourself. Here's the very last map in the whole flaming atlas! We went off that over an hour ago!' He turned the page. As in all atlases, there were two completely blank pages at the very end. 'So now we must be somewhere here,' he said, putting a finger on one of the blank pages.

'Where's here?' cried the Head of the Army.

The young pilot was still grinning broadly. He said to them, 'That's why they always put two blank pages at the back of the atlas. They're for new countries. You're meant to fill them in yourself.'

The Head of the Air Force glanced down at the ground below. 'Just look at this godforsaken desert!' he cried. 'All the trees are dead and all the rocks are blue!'

'The giant has stopped,' the young pilot said. 'He's waving us down.'

The pilots throttled back the engines and all nine helicopters landed safely on the great yellow wasteland. Then each of them lowered a ramp from its belly. Nine jeeps, one from each helicopter, were driven down the ramps. Each jeep contained six soldiers and a vast quantity of thick rope and heavy chains.

'I don't see any giants,' the Head of the Army said.

'The giants is all just out of sight over there,' the BFG told him. 'But if you is taking these sloshbuckling noisy

186

bellypoppers any closer, all the giants is waking up at once and then pop goes the weasel.'

'So you want us to proceed by jeep?' the Head of the Army said.

'Yes,' the BFG said. 'But you must all be very very hushy quiet. No roaring of motors. No shouting. No mucking about. No piggery-jokery.'

The BFG, with Sophie still in his ear, trotted forward and the jeeps followed close behind.

Suddenly the most dreadful rumbling noise was heard by everyone. The Head of the Army went pea-green in the face. 'Those are guns!' he cried. 'There is a battle raging somewhere up ahead of us! Turn back, the lot of you! Let's get out of here!'

'Pigspiffle!' the BFG said. 'Those noises is not guns.'

'Of course they're guns!' shouted the Head of the Army. 'I am a military man and I know a gun when I hear one! Turn back!'

'Those is just the giants snortling in their sleep,' the BFG said. 'I is a giant myself and I know a giant's snortle when I is hearing one.'

'Are you quite sure?' the Army man said anxiously.

'Positive,' the BFG said.

'Proceed cautiously,' the Army man ordered.

They all moved on.

Then they saw them!

Even at a distance, they were enough to scare the daylights out of the soldiers. But when they got close and saw what the giants really looked like, they began to sweat with fear. Nine fearsome, ugly, half-naked, fifty-feet-long brutes lay sprawled over the ground in various

grotesque attitudes of sleep, and the sound of their snoring was indeed like gunfire in a battle.

The BFG raised a hand. The jeeps all stopped. The soldiers got out.

'What happens if one of them wakes up?' whispered the Head of the Army, his knees knocking together from fear.

'If any one of them is waking up, he will gobble you down before you can say knack jife,' the BFG answered, grinning hugely. 'Me is the only one what won't be gobbled up because giants is never eating giants. Me and Sophie is the only safe ones because I is hiding her if that happens.'

The Head of the Army took several paces to the rear. So did the Head of the Air Force. They climbed rather quickly back into their jeep, ready to make a fast getaway if necessary. 'Go forward, men!' the Head of the Army said. 'Go forward and do your duty bravely!'

The soldiers crept forward with their ropes and chains. All of them were trembling mightily. None dared speak a word.

The BFG, with Sophie now sitting on the palm of his hand, stood near by watching the operation.

To give the soldiers their due, they were extremely courageous. There were six well-trained efficient men working on each giant and within ten minutes eight out of the nine giants had been trussed up like chickens and were still snoring contentedly. The ninth, who happened to be the Fleshlumpeater, was causing trouble for the soldiers because he was lying with his right arm tucked underneath his enormous body. It was impossible to tie his wrists and arms together without first getting that arm out from underneath him.

Very very cautiously, the six soldiers who were working on the Fleshlumpeater began to pull at the huge arm, trying to release it. The Fleshlumpeater opened his tiny piggy black eyes.

'Which of you foulpesters is wiggling my arm?' he bellowed. 'Is that you, you rotsome Manhugger?'

Suddenly he saw the soldiers. In a flash, he was sitting up. He looked around him. He saw more soldiers. With a roar, he leapt to his feet. The soldiers, petrified with fear, froze where they were. They had no weapons with them. The Head of the Army put his jeep into reverse.

'Human beans!' the Flushlumpeater yelled. 'What is all you flushbunking rotsome half-baked beans doing in our country?' He made a grab at a soldier and swept him up in his hand.

'I is having early suppers today!' he shouted, holding the poor squirming soldier at arm's length and roaring with laughter.

Sophie, standing on the palm of the BFG's hand, was watching horrorstruck. 'Do something!' she cried.

'Quick, before he eats him!'

'Put that human bean down!' the BFG shouted.

The Fleshlumpeater turned and stared at the BFG. 'What is *you* doing here with all these grotty twiglets!' he bellowed. 'You is making me very suspichy!'

The BFG made a rush at the Fleshlumpeater, but the colossal fifty-four-foot-high giant simply knocked him over with a flick of his free arm. At the same time, Sophie fell off the BFG's palm on to the ground. Her mind was racing. She *must* do something! She *must!* She *must!* She remembered the sapphire brooch the Queen had pinned on to her chest. Quickly, she undid it.

'I is guzzling you nice and slow!' the Fleshlumpeater was saying to the soldier in his hand. 'Then I is guzzling ten or twenty more of you midgy little maggots down there! You is not getting away from me because I is galloping fifty times faster than you!'

Sophie ran up behind the Fleshlumpeater. She was holding the brooch between her fingers. When she was right up close to the great naked hairy legs, she rammed the three-inch long pin of the brooch as hard as she could into the Fleshlumpeater's right ankle. It went deep into the flesh and stayed there.

The giant gave a roar of pain and jumped high in the air. He dropped the soldier and made a grab for his ankle.

The BFG, knowing what a coward the Fleshlump-eater was, saw his chance. 'You is bitten by a snake!' he shouted. 'I seed it biting you! It was a frightsome poisnowse viper! It was a dreadly dungerous vindscreen viper!'

'Save our souls!' bellowed the Fleshlumpeater. 'Sound the crumpets! I is bitten by a septicous venomsome vindscreen viper!' He flopped to the ground and sat there howling his head off and clutching his ankle with both hands. His fingers felt the brooch. 'The teeth of the dreadly viper is still sticking into me!' he yelled. 'I is feeling the teeth sticking into my anklet!'

The BFG saw his second chance. 'We must be getting those viper's teeth out at once!' he cried. 'Otherwise you is deader than duck-soup! I is helping you!'

The BFG knelt down beside the Fleshlumpeater. 'You must grab your anklet very tight with both hands!' he ordered. 'That will stop the poisnowse juices from the venomsome viper going up your leg and into your heart!'

The Fleshlumpeater grabbed his ankle with both hands.

'Now close your eyes and grittle your teeth and look up to heaven and say your prayers while I is taking out the teeth of the venomsome viper,' the BFG said.

The terrified Fleshlumpeater did exactly as he was told.

The BFG signalled for some rope. A soldier rushed it over to him. With both the Fleshlumpeater's hands gripping his ankle, it was a simple matter for the BFG to tie the ankles and hands together with a tight knot.

'I is pulling out the frightsome viper's teeth!' the BFG said as he pulled the knot tight.

'Do it quickly!' shouted the Fleshlumpeater, 'before I is pizzened to death!'

'There we is,' said the BFG, standing up. 'You can look now.'

When the Fleshlumpeater saw that he was trussed up like a turkey, he gave a yell so loud that the heavens trembled. He rolled and he wriggled, he fought and he figgled, he squirmed and he squiggled. But there was not a thing he could do.

'Well done you!' Sophie cried.

'Well done *you!*' said the BFG, smiling down at the little girl. 'You is saving all of our lives!'

'Will you please get that brooch back for me,' Sophie said. 'It belongs to the Queen.'

The BFG pulled the beautiful brooch out of the Flesh-lumpeater's ankle. The Fleshlumpeater howled. The

BFG wiped the pin and handed it back to Sophie.

Curiously, not one of the other eight snoring giants had woken up during this shimozzle. 'When you is only sleeping one or two hours a day, you is sleeping extra doubly deep,' the BFG explained.

The Heads of the Army and the Air Force drove forward once again in their jeep. 'Her Majesty will be very pleased with me,' the Head of the Army said. 'I shall probably get a medal. What's the next move?'

'Now you is all driving over to my cave to load up my bottles of dreams,' the BFG said.

'We can't waste time with that rubbish,' the Army General said.

'It is the Queen's order,' Sophie said. She was now back on the BFG's hand.

So the nine jeeps drove across to the BFG's cave and the great dream-loading operation began. There were fifty-thousand jars in all to be loaded up, more than five thousand to each jeep, and it took over an hour to finish the job.

While the soldiers were loading the dreams, the BFG and Sophie disappeared over the mountains on a mysterious errand. When they came back, the BFG had a sack the size of a small house slung over his shoulder.

'What's that you've got in there?' the Head of the Army demanded to know.

'Curiosity is killing the rat,' the BFG said, and he turned away from the silly man.

When he was sure that all his precious dreams had been safely loaded on to the jeeps, the BFG said, 'Now we is driving back to the bellypoppers and picking up the frightsome giants.'

The jeeps drove back to the helicopters. The fifty thousand dreams were carried carefully, jar by jar, on to the helicopters. The soldiers climbed back on board, but the B F G and Sophie stayed on the ground. Then they all returned to where the nine giants were lying.

It was a fine sight to see them, these great air machines hovering over the trussed-up giants. It was an even finer sight to see the giants being woken up by the terrific thundering of the engines overhead, and the finest sight of all was to observe those nine hideous brutes squirming and twisting about on the ground like a mass of mighty snakes as they tried to free themselves from their ropes and chains.

'I is flushbunkled!' roared the Fleshlumpeater.
'I is splitzwiggled!' yelled the Childchewer.
'I is swogswalloped!' bellowed the Bonecruncher.
'I is goosegruggled!' howled the Manhugger.
'I is gunzleswiped!' shouted the Meatdripper.
'I is fluckgungled!' screamed the Maidmasher.
'I is slopgroggled!' squawked the Gizzardgulper.
'I is crodsquinkled!' yowled the Bloodbottler.
'I is bopmuggered!' screeched the Butcher Boy.

The nine giant-carrying helicopters each chose a separate giant and hovered directly over him. Very strong steel hawsers with hooks on the ends of them were lowered from the front and rear of each helicopter. The BFG quickly secured the hooks to the giants' chains, one hook near the legs and the other near the arms. Then very slowly, the giants were winched up into the air, parallel with the ground. The giants roared and bellowed, but there was nothing they could do.

The BFG, with Sophie once more resting comfortably in his ear, set off at a gallop for England. The helicopters all banked around and followed after him.

It was an amazing spectacle, those nine helicopters winging through the sky, each with a trussed-up fifty-foot-long giant slung underneath it. The giants themselves must have found it an interesting experience. They never stopped bellowing, but their howls were drowned by the noise of the engines.

When it began to get dark, the helicopters switched on powerful searchlights and trained them on to the galloping giant so as to keep him in sight. They flew right through the night and arrived in England just as dawn was breaking.

Feeding Time

While the giants were being captured, a tremendous bustle and hustle was going on back home in England. Every earth-digger and mechanical contrivance in the country had been mobilized to dig the colossal hole in which the nine giants were to be permanently imprisoned.

Ten thousand men and ten thousand machines worked ceaselessly through the night under powerful arc-lights, and the massive task was completed only just in time.

The hole itself was about twice the size of a football field and five hundred feet deep. The walls were perpendicular and engineers had calculated that there was no way a giant could escape once he was put in. Even if all nine giants were to stand on each other's shoulders, the topmost giant would still be some fifty feet from the top of the hole.

The nine giant-carrying helicopters hovered over the massive pit. The giants, one by one, were lowered to the floor. But they were still trussed up and now came the tricky business of releasing them from their bonds. Nobody wanted to go down and do this because the moment a giant was freed, he would be sure to turn on the wretched person who had freed him and gobble him up.

As usual, the BFG had the answer. 'I has told you

before,' he said, 'giants is never eating giants, so I is going down and I shall untie them myself before you can say rack jobinson.'

With thousands of fascinated spectators, including the Queen, peering down into the pit, the BFG was lowered on a rope. One by one, he released the giants. They stood up, stretched their stiffened limbs and started leaping about in fury.

'Why is they putting us down here in this grobsludging hole?' they shouted at the BFG.

'Because you is guzzling human beans,' the BFG answered. 'I is always warning you not to do it and you is never taking the titchiest bit of notice.'

'In that case,' the Fleshlumpeater bellowed, 'I think we is guzzling *you* instead!'

The BFG grabbed the dangling rope and was hoisted out of the pit just in time.

The great bulging sack he had brought back with him from Giant Country lay at the top of the pit.

'What's in there?' the Queen asked him.

The BFG put an arm into the sack and pulled out a gigantic black and white striped object the size of a man.

'Snozzcumbers!' he cried. 'This is the repulsant snozzcumber, Majester, and that is all we is going to give these disgustive giants from now on!'

'May I taste it?' the Queen asked.

'Don't, Majester, don't!' cried the BFG. 'It is tasting of trogfilth and pigsquibble!' With that he tossed the snozzcumber down to the giants below. 'There's your supper!' he shouted. 'Have a munch on that!' He fished out more snozzcumbers from the sack and threw them

down. The giants below howled and cursed. The BFG laughed. 'It serves them right left and centre!' he said.

'What will we feed them on when the snozzcumbers are all used up?' the Queen asked him.

'They is never being used up, Majester,' the BFG answered, smiling. 'I is also bringing in this sack a whole bungle of snozzcumber plants which I is giving, with your permission, to the royal gardener to put in the soil. Then we is having an everlasting supply of this repulsant food to feed these thirstbloody giants on.'

'What a clever fellow you are,' the Queen said. 'You are not very well educated but you are really nobody's fool, I can see that.'

The Author

Every country in the world that had in the past been visited by the foul man-eating giants sent telegrams of congratulations and thanks to the BFG and to Sophie. Kings and Presidents and Prime Ministers and Rulers of every kind showered the enormous giant and the little girl with compliments and thank-yous, as well as all sorts of medals and presents.

The Ruler of India sent the BFG a magnificent elephant, the very thing he had been wishing for all his life.

The King of Arabia sent them a camel each.

The Lama of Tibet sent them a llama each.

Wellington sent them one hundred pairs of wellies each.

Panama sent them beautiful hats.

The King of Sweden sent them a barrelful of sweet and sour pork.

Jersey sent them pullovers.

There was no end to the gratitude of the world.

The Queen herself gave orders that a special house with tremendous high ceilings and enormous doors should immediately be built in Windsor Great Park, next to her own castle, for the BFG to live in. And a pretty little cottage was put up next door for Sophie. The BFG's house was to have a special dream-storing room with hundreds of shelves in it where he could put his beloved bottles. What is more, he was given the title of The Royal Dream-Blower. He was allowed to go galloping off to any place in England on any night of the year to blow his splendid phizzwizards in through the windows to sleeping children. And letters poured into his house by the million from children begging him to pay them a visit.

Meanwhile, tourists from all over the globe came flocking to gaze down in wonder at the nine horrendous man-eating giants in the great pit. They came especially at feeding-time, when the snozzcumbers were being thrown down to them by the keeper, and it was a pleasure

NOTICE

IT IS FORBIDDEN
TO FEED
THE GIANTS

by order
Keeper

to listen to the howls and growls of horror coming up from the pit as the giants began to chew upon the filthiest-tasting vegetable on earth.

There was only one disaster. Three silly men who had drunk too much beer for lunch decided to climb over the high fence surrounding the pit, and of course they fell in. There were yells of delight from the giants below, followed by the crunching of bones. The head keeper immediately put up a big notice on the fence saying, IT IS FORBIDDEN TO FEED THE GIANTS. And after that, there were no more disasters.

The BFG expressed a wish to learn how to speak properly, and Sophie herself, who loved him as she would a father, volunteered to give him lessons every day. She even taught him how to spell and to write sentences, and he turned out to be a splendid intelligent pupil. In his spare time, he read books. He became a tremendous reader. He read all of Charles Dickens (whom he no longer called Dahl's Chickens), and all of Shakespeare and literally thousands of other books. He also started to write essays about his own past life. When Sophie read some of them, she said, 'These are very good. I think perhaps one day you could become a real writer.'

'Oh, I would love that!' cried the BFG. 'Do you think I could?'

'I know you could,' Sophie said. 'Why don't you start by writing a book about you and me?'

'Very well,' the BFG said. 'I'll give it a try.'

So he did. He worked hard on it and in the end he completed it. Rather shyly, he showed it to the Queen. The Queen read it aloud to her grandchildren. Then the Queen said, 'I think we ought to get this book printed properly and published so that other children can read it.' This was arranged, but because the BFG was a very modest giant, he wouldn't put his own name on it. He used somebody else's name instead.

But where, you might ask, is this book that the BFG wrote?

It's right here. You've just finished reading it.

Read more from ROALD DAHL, the World's No. 1 Storyteller!

Willy Wonka's famous chocolate factory is opening at last!

But only five lucky children will be allowed inside. And the winners are: Augustus Gloop, an enormously fat boy whose hobby is eating; Veruca Salt, a spoiled-rotten brat whose parents are wrapped around her little finger; Violet Beauregarde, a dim-witted gum-chewer with the fastest jaws around; Mike Teavee, a toy pistol–toting gangster-in-training who is obsessed with television; and Charlie Bucket, Our Hero, a boy who is honest and kind, brave and true, and good and ready for the wildest time of his life!

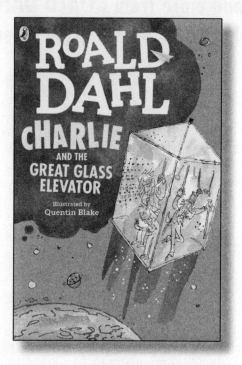

Now that he's won the chocolate factory, what's next for Charlie?

Last seen flying through the sky in a giant elevator in *Charlie and the Chocolate Factory*, Charlie Bucket's back for another adventure. When the giant elevator picks up speed, Charlie, Willy Wonka, and the gang are sent hurtling through space and time. Visiting the world's first space hotel, battling the dreaded Vermicious Knids, and saving the world are only a few stops along this remarkable, intergalactic joyride.

"The Trunchbull" is no match for Matilda!

Matilda is a sweet, exceptional young girl, but her parents think she's just a nuisance. She expects school to be different, but there she has to face Miss Trunchbull, a kid-hating terror of a headmistress. When Matilda is attacked by the Trunchbull, she suddenly discovers she has a remarkable power with which to fight back. It'll take a superhuman genius to give Miss Trunchbull what she deserves, and Matilda may be just the one to do it!

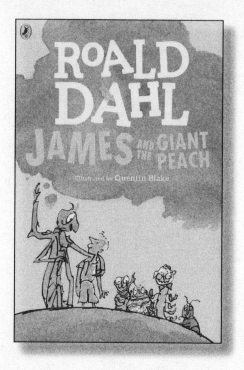

A little magic can take you a long way!

After James Henry Trotter's parents are tragically eaten by a rhinoceros, he goes to live with his two horrible aunts, Spiker and Sponge. Life there is no fun, until James accidentally drops some magic crystals by the old peach tree and strange things start to happen. The peach at the top of the tree begins to grow, and before long it's as big as a house. Inside, James meets a bunch of oversized friends—Grasshopper, Centipede, Ladybug, and more. With a snip of the stem, the peach starts rolling away, and the great adventure begins!

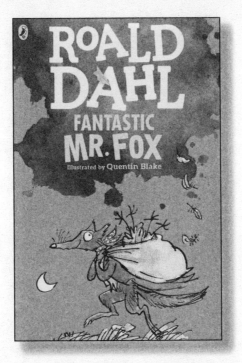

Nobody outfoxes Fantastic Mr. Fox!

Someone's been stealing from the three meanest farmers around, and they know the identity of the thief—it's Fantastic Mr. Fox! Working alone they could never catch him; but now fat Boggis, squat Bunce, and skinny Bean have joined forces, and they have Mr. Fox and his family surrounded. What they don't know is that they're not dealing with just any fox—Mr. Fox would rather die than surrender. Only the most fantastic plan can save him now.

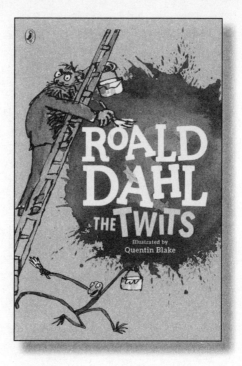

How do you outwit a Twit?

Mr. and Mrs. Twit are the smelliest, nastiest, ugliest people in the world. They hate everything—except playing mean jokes on each other, catching innocent birds to put in their Bird Pies, and making their caged monkeys, the Muggle-Wumps, stand on their heads all day. But the Muggle-Wumps have had enough. They don't just want out, they want revenge.

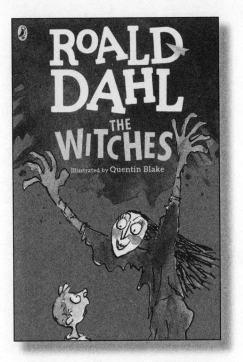

This is not a fairy tale.
This is about *real* witches.

Grandmamma loves to tell about witches. Real witches
are the most dangerous of all living creatures on earth.
There's nothing they hate so much as children, and they
work all kinds of terrifying spells to get rid of them. Her
grandson listens closely to Grandmamma's stories—but
nothing can prepare him for the day he comes face-to-
face with The Grand High Witch herself!

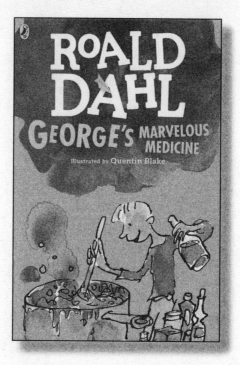

A taste of her own medicine.

George is alone in the house with Grandma. The most
horrid, grizzly old grunion of a grandma ever. She needs
something stronger than her usual medicine to cure her
grouchiness. A special grandma medicine, a remedy
for *everything*. And George knows just what to put into
it. Grandma's in for the surprise of her life—and so is
George, when he sees the results of his mixture!

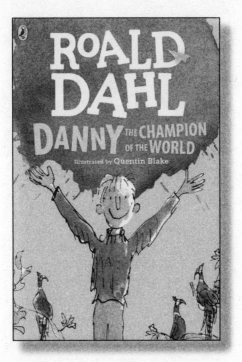

Can Danny and his father outsmart the villainous Mr. Hazell?

Danny has a life any boy would love—his home is a gypsy caravan, he's the youngest master car mechanic around, and his best friend is his dad, who never runs out of wonderful stories to tell. But one night Danny discovers a shocking secret that his father has kept hidden for years. Soon Danny finds himself the mastermind behind the most incredible plot ever attempted against nasty Victor Hazell, a wealthy landowner with a bad attitude. Can they pull it off? If so, Danny will truly be the champion of the world.

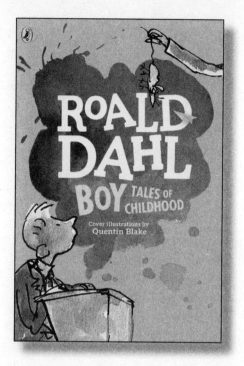

Where did Roald Dahl get all of his wonderful ideas for stories?

From his own life, of course! As full of excitement and the unexpected as his world-famous, bestselling books, Roald Dahl's tales of his own childhood are completely fascinating and fiendishly funny. Did you know that Roald Dahl nearly lost his nose in a car accident? Or that he was once a chocolate candy tester for Cadbury's? Have you heard about his involvement in the Great Mouse Plot of 1924? If not, you don't yet know all there is to know about Roald Dahl. Sure to captivate and delight you, the boyhood antics of this master storyteller are not to be missed!

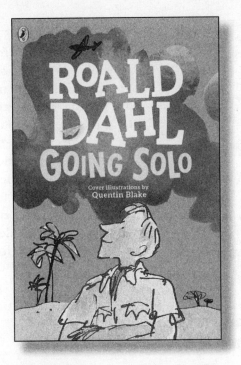

Superb stories, daring deeds, fantastic adventures!

Going Solo is the action-packed tale of Roald Dahl's exploits as a World War II pilot. Learn all about his encounters with the enemy, his worldwide travels, the life-threatening injuries he sustained in a plane accident, and the rest of his sometimes bizarre, often unnerving, and always colorful adventures. Told with the same irresistible appeal that has made Roald Dahl one of the world's best-loved writers, *Going Solo* brings you directly into the action and into the mind of this fascinating man.

Look out, kids!

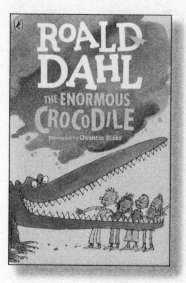

The Enormous Crocodile is incredibly hungry—and incredibly greedy. His favorite meal is a plump, juicy little child, and he intends to gobble up as many of them as he can! He is sure that his "secret plans and clever tricks" cannot be foiled. But when the other animals in the jungle join together to put an end to his wicked schemes, the Enormous Crocodile learns a lesson he won't soon forget.

What happens when the hunter becomes the hunted?

To the Gregg family, hunting is just plain fun. To the girl who lives next door, it's just plain horrible. She tries to be polite. She tries to talk them out of it, but the Greggs only laugh at her. Then one day the Greggs go too far, and the little girl turns her Magic Finger on them. When she's very, very angry, the little girl's Magic Finger takes over. She really can't control it, and now it's turned the Greggs into birds! Before they know it, the Greggs are living in a nest, and that's just the beginning of their problems . . .

Who needs a ladder when you've got a giraffe with an extended neck?

The Ladderless Window-Cleaning Company certainly doesn't. They don't need a pail, either, because they have a pelican with a bucket-sized beak. With a monkey to do the washing and Billy as their manager, this business is destined for success. Now they have their big break—a chance to clean all 677 windows of the Hampshire House, owned by the richest man in all of England! That's exciting enough, but along the way there are surprises and adventures beyond their wildest window-washing dreams.

n ancient spell, 140 tortoises, and a little bit of magic . . .

r. Hoppy is in love with his neighbor, Mrs. Silver; but she is in love with someone else—Alfie, her pet rtoise. With all her attention focused on Alfie, Mrs. Silver doesn't en know Mr. Hoppy is alive. And r. Hoppy is too shy to even ask rs. Silver over for tea. Then one y Mr. Hoppy comes up with a rilliant idea to get Mrs. Silver's attion. If Mr. Hoppy's plan works, rs. Silver will certainly fall in ve with him. After all, everyone nows the way to a woman's heart through her tortoise.

STORIES ARE GOOD FOR YOU.

Roald Dahl said,
"If you have good thoughts, they will shine out of your face like sunbeams and you will always look lovely."

We believe in doing good things.
That's why 10 percent of all Roald Dahl income* goes to our charity partners. We have supported causes including: specialist children's nurses, grants for families in need, and educational outreach programs. Thank you for helping us to sustain this vital work.

Find out more at roalddahl.com

The Roald Dahl Charitable Trust is a registered UK charity (no. 1119330).
* All author payments and royalty income net of third-party commissions.